PRAISE FOR J. F. ENGLERT'S

A DOG ABOUT TOWN

"Randolph is fantastic as he uses his canine sense and intelligence to find the killer."
—*Midwest Book Review*

"A cliff-hanger at the end makes me hope for a sequel. . . . I felt like Randolph could be a friend, and look forward to meeting him again."
—*Deadly Pleasures*

"A refreshingly intelligent story told from the perspective of a dog . . . an entertaining who-done-it . . . Cozy mystery fans will enjoy this unique, well-written tale."
—*Freshfiction.com*

A DOG AMONG DIPLOMATS

A Bull Moose Dog Run Mystery

J. F. ENGLERT

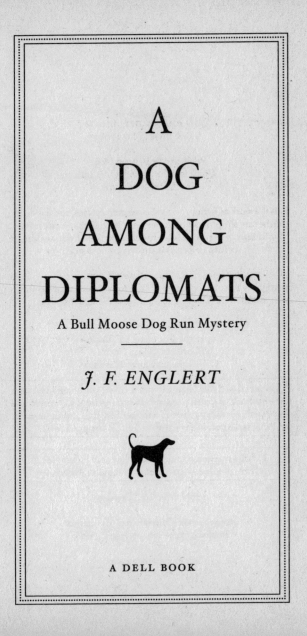

A DELL BOOK

A DOG AMONG DIPLOMATS
A Dell Book / May 2008

Published by Bantam Dell
A Division of Random House, Inc.
New York, New York

This is a work of fiction. Names, characters, places, and incidents
either are the product of the author's imagination or are used
fictitiously. Any resemblance to actual persons, living or dead,
events, or locales is entirely coincidental.

Dell is a registered trademark of Random House, Inc.,
and the colophon is a trademark of Random House, Inc.

ISBN 978-0-440-24364-9

Printed in the United States of America
Published simultaneously in Canada

www.bantamdell.com

OPM   10 9 8 7 6 5 4 3 2 1

For Penelope

Acknowledgments

J. F. Englert would like to thank Danielle Perez for her fine editorial counsel; everyone at Bantam Dell for their work, both practical and artistic; Susan Stava for her photography; Jamie Block for his music and permission to use his lyrics in the epigraph; Claudia Cross and Marcy Posner at Sterling Lord Literistic for making sure that Randolph found a good home both in the United States and abroad; and Catherine and Dulcie for their kind walk-on into Randolph's world.

The Queen of 5th St.
Holds court in a one-room flat.
The jewels of state in a shoebox,
The Dog's the Diplomat.
And the stars on the ceiling
They change once a year.
Makes her feel like she's touring
Another hemisphere.

—from "Queen of 5th St."
by Jamie Block

A
DOG
AMONG
DIPLOMATS

IT'S NOT EVERY DAY THAT a young man clad only in boxer shorts embossed with red hearts dies beneath an opened parachute in a small third-floor room in one of New York's last boardinghouses. It's even rarer that a visual artist, the owner of a Labrador retriever equipped with a generous belly, a fine mind and an admirable temperament, is called to the scene by the police department before the body is even cold. Yet this is exactly what happened just after ten p.m. on a recent mild March night.

I was sitting on my haunches in our cozy apartment on the Upper West Side of Manhattan, looking into the middle distance and allowing a mother lode of Chinese spareribs to settle pleasantly in my gullet. I felt a postdinner nap coming on and was not planning to resist (in this hectic world it is often a struggle to get my twelve-hour sleep quota). Harry, my twenty-something owner, was beginning the third hour of a documentary on the life of Vincent van Gogh, narrated, it seemed, by a narcoleptic whose voice rose at all the wrong moments, as if he had just been poked awake again in the sound booth.

Then the phone rang. My owner had already taken me for my evening Numbers 1 and 2 (shortchanging himself van Gogh's contentious roommateship with Gauguin at Arles) and was loath to be roused from Grandfather Oswald's La-Z-Boy for anything short of an evacuation of Manhattan for the apocalypse. He let the machine pick up, and Imogen's voice filled our living room.

"Leave a message after the beep," she said before trailing off into an uncertain whisper. "Harry, is it a beep?"

The mild but decisive voice of the caller came next.

"Harry, it's Detective Davis. If you're there, pick up. It's important. It involves . . . her."

Harry flew out of his La-Z-Boy recliner and grabbed the phone. My nose could detect the strong waves of hope, excitement and possibility that my owner shed. I wondered if Detective Peter Davis, the lead investigator in Imogen's case, had a breakthrough to report. Our lovely

Imogen, who had rescued me from the pet-store clods and then included Harry in our domestic arrangements, had disappeared over a year before without a word or lead—foul play suspected. I had not yet informed Harry, but I had spotted her once again disappearing into a subway tunnel after the successful—if brutal—conclusion to our last mystery. That investigation had pushed both Harry and me to great extremes of endurance and ingenuity, and the end found us on the verge of an even larger mystery, which promised to span the globe in a conspiratorial and high-stakes web before it brought some resolution to our loss of Imogen. Detective Davis's phone call was the beginning of what would prove to be Act II.

"I'm here," Harry said into the receiver, then listened without a word. He found a pen amid a pile of paintbrushes on the side table and scribbled down an address.

"Okay, Peter. I'll be there in twenty minutes."

My owner hung up the phone, grabbed a light jacket and disappeared through the door and down the stairs without a word to his dog. The peace was shattered—what is peace if it can be broken so easily?—and all prospects of an after-dinner nap seemed to vanish in the face of this fresh anxiety. But fortunately I am built to endure, and soon the soporific magic of the spareribs began to affect me and I closed my eyes for a dreamless snooze.

Let me now share with you the particular facts that mark my existence. I am a Labrador retriever who lives in Manhattan, the isle of my birth, to which I am deeply attached. I am also sentient. Other dogs might be as well, to a greater or lesser degree, but few take pleasure from reading the important works of your human literature or make expansive journeys of imagination as Yours Truly does. I am self-taught, having learned to read from the pages of New York's finest tabloid newspapers laid out for my house-training. The writers, particularly those responsible for headlines, are the unheralded poets of our age (by way of evidence, the *Post*'s sublime: HEADLESS BODY FOUND IN TOPLESS BAR). Lest I lose myself in the sometimes lurid virtues of the tabloid, the main challenge of this Labrador's life is the fact that his prodigious brain—2.3 pounds of smoothly functioning gelatinous gray matter—is trapped within a body as unresponsive to the nuances of thought as a piece of chocolate (a delicacy I am supposed to avoid because my liver cannot handle it). Because of this physical "frozenness," I cannot express in any facial gesture what I am thinking.

Blankness is my trademark, though many humans describe my eyes as "soulful." My tail has a life of its own and wags idiotically even when I am in a black mood. Then there is an involuntary body tremble that my owner frequently mistakes for bladder-based urgency because it jingles the tags on my collar (not that I am ever ungrateful for regular outings to the sidewalks, dog runs or parks of New York). Owners, please never underestimate the importance of liberal access to Numbers 1 and 2 — no need to make us test our house-trained credentials.

Being unable to choose when I can relieve myself and under what conditions is symbolic of the many restrictions in my life. I cannot, for example, simply walk out the front door of our apartment and wander the streets without a human chaperone. For most of my relatively short life (I will be six in November) I have not minded these restrictions. I have had wonderful people to whom I belonged and who belonged to me. I have had my books and a cozy corner in which to discreetly enjoy them, to listen to the wind or the rain on the drainpipe and mull over the wisdom of the classics and the music of words.

But then Imogen disappeared and people died and I needed to apply whatever strengths I had to protecting my owner and learning the truth. Prior to this development I had always steered clear of trying to communicate with humans. As warm as my relations are with Harry, I never trusted the species as a whole. There is always some P. T. Barnum in the woodwork, ready to try to make a buck from the latest animal freak, or, worse still, an overly zealous scientist eager to shave off every inch of a Labrador's fur and snap on the electrodes to prove that we are a higher form of life. No thank you. But despite my reluctance to "shine," the necessities of protecting my owner and solving a mystery required that I construct a bridge between species. I did this by using Harry's favorite cereal, Alpha-Bits, and composing messages from "beyond" out of the friendly little letters. Harry is susceptible to the idea of the paranormal. Ghosts, spirits, communication from beyond now make up part of his worldview. Someday, I hope, this irrational fever will pass, but we all nurse our wounds differently and losing Imogen was a harsh blow. For my part, I stick to reason and those elements of intuition and dog sense that have helped me navigate this life. Perhaps I stick to these things a little too much. The point, though, is that I used Harry's susceptibility as a way to introduce the messages I wrote and make them credible. The messages came from a spirit guide whom I dubbed Holmes. My uncritical owner left the stone unturned and I was never found out, even though near the end I had Holmes indicate that I had been "inspired" and that my owner should follow my lead.

Harry returned to our apartment after three hours, and I awoke from my after-dinner slumber to find him smoking one of his emergency cigarettes as he came through the door. Things were clearly very grim.

Fortunately, my owner often gives voice to his recent experiences and thus keeps his dog well informed. The following is a narrative of what transpired after Harry left our apartment, which I have pieced together from his reiteration of events and information I gathered soon after.

My owner had taken a taxi to the address provided by Detective Davis. He stepped out of the cab to find himself standing before a large redbrick residential building in the East Village. Most of the windows were dark, but one room on the third floor was ablaze with light, and Harry saw figures appear and disappear in the window: a man with a tape measure; someone else in a big white suit with a face mask. It was a forensics team collecting evidence.

"No one in. No one out," a police officer said. He stood between Harry and the entrance to the building.

"Detective Davis told me to come," Harry said.

The policeman stepped aside. Harry climbed a short flight of stairs and, entering through the open front door, found himself in the lobby of what could have been mistaken for a New England bed-and-breakfast if it were not filled with an oddly incongruous bunch of foreign nationals, drag queens and vagrants.

"Wow," Harry muttered as he absorbed the scene.

Rough-and-tumble bachelor-athlete type though Harry may be, even my owner knows that doilies, woven wicker baskets, plastic cornucopias with waxy grapes do not typically belong in the East Village and definitely not with this pirate crew.

"They're the residents," Detective Davis said from the landing of the interior staircase. He spoke loudly, as if he wanted everyone to hear. "Come on upstairs, Harry."

Harry did as he was told and began to climb the several flights of stairs to the third floor.

"Interesting place," Harry said. "What is it?"

"A boardinghouse," Detective Davis said. "Probably one of the last ones in Manhattan. There used to be hundreds, thousands even. Then they turned most of them into SROs— single-resident-occupancy buildings—but not this one. This one is classic Bowery bum."

"Yeah, the people don't really seem to fit," Harry said as they climbed the stairs, occasionally brushing past crime-scene personnel carrying clear plastic bags filled with suspicious-looking contents gathered up above on the third floor. "I mean, there's a complimentary coffee and tea station. There's a fire going in the fireplace. There're Currier and Ives prints on the wall."

"Some of those aren't prints," Detective Davis said in hushed tones. "Let me give you the short version. Ten years ago this place was a dump. A gun cage around reception. Dealers on the stoop. Graffiti all over that wall where the Currier and Ives are now. Then two things happened: the neighborhood started to improve, and the lady who owns the place won the lottery. Instead of doing what most people would with the winnings—buy a villa in Tuscany, sail the world—she decided to renovate the place."

"I got it," Harry concluded. "But she couldn't

get rid of the old tenants. That explains the people downstairs."

"No," Detective Davis said as they arrived at the third floor. "She didn't *want* to get rid of the tenants. She wanted to give them a taste of the good life too. Harry, I think that she is either one of the craziest women on the planet or the happiest. Most of the time I lean toward thinking she's the happiest. After all, only the happiest sort of person would win all of that money and not leave their past behind. Only the happiest sort of person has that kind of peace."

He paused.

"Now let's go look at the corpse."

Detective Davis motioned for the forensics team to clear the room, and two men and one woman in sanitary jumpsuits promptly exited with more bags of evidence. Harry moved as if to cover his nose the way he had seen in detective shows, but Davis intervened.

"No need. There's no smell. If he's been dead more than two hours I'd be surprised. Forensics will tell us soon enough."

Harry stood just inside the room and looked around. At first there was not much to see: a queen-sized bed, a writing desk and desk lamp, a waist-high chest of drawers and two large klieg lights brought by the police to illuminate the room. Then Harry saw the legs sticking out between the bed and the window. The legs ended in the white boxer shorts embossed with red hearts. The rest of the body was covered by a gently inflated white parachute that draped from the bed onto the floor like the roof of a child's tent playhouse.

"You haven't moved it yet?" Harry asked.

"Oh, yeah. We moved it, but I had them put it back."

"For me?" Harry asked.

"For me," Detective Davis said. "I like to freeze the scene in my mind. It helps me trace backward if I know how it all finally ended."

"Sounds like a meditation."

"Only when the bodies don't stink or someone's not shooting a gun at you or swinging a machete."

"The parachute's strange," Harry observed.

"The parachute's a real winner. The touch of the poet," Detective Davis said. "He didn't die falling off his bed. He was strangled with the parachute cord. He's a strong young man. Very fit. But there isn't a sign of a struggle. People don't let themselves get strangled. They kick. They punch. They scratch. They fight. The only time they don't is when they aren't conscious to begin with. Whoever did this first made sure he wasn't conscious. He was probably drugged. I'd guess chloral hydrate. We found two champagne glasses and a bottle—Schramsberg—the California bubbly Richard Nixon used to toast détente with China in the seventies. It's all being tested now, but I can already tell you what they'll find. Powerful sleeping agent in only one of the glasses and plenty of DNA over everything…"

"I don't get it, Peter. What's this got to do with Imogen?"

Detective Davis motioned toward the dresser, which was bare except for a large photo frame.

"Take a look at those pictures."

The frame contained two photographs, one above the other. Both featured our mistress. The top photograph showed Imogen in a red cocktail dress, smiling broadly. The bottom photograph showed my mistress and Yours Truly, but I will save further description of the picture because it was the top photograph that gripped my owner now. In it, Imogen's arm was around the shoulder of a young man. Her hair was short, as it had been when I had last seen her racing toward the subway.

"My God. It's her," Harry whispered. Harry reached to pick up the frame and hold it close, but Detective Davis stopped him.

"Harry, please don't touch. It's evidence."

"Who's that guy?"

"That guy is *that* guy," Detective Davis said, pointing at the body beneath the parachute. "Beyond that I couldn't tell you. I was hoping that you could tell me."

"I've never seen him before," Harry said. "But Imogen looks so different."

"Short hair," Detective Davis said. "Is that it?"

"I've never seen the dress," Harry said. "It's very un-Imogen. She was a jeans and T-shirt girl."

"So you think the photograph is recent?"

"Excuse me?"

"That it was taken after she disappeared…"

"What?"

Harry could not grasp the meaning of Detective Davis's words, because, as I mentioned above, I had not yet informed him that Imogen was alive. There was no "after she disappeared" for Harry. In Harry's mind, Imogen had no "after" life that did not include him. Harry was of two minds: Imogen was dead, but, because he loved her beyond telling, she never could be. She haunted him but was permanently frozen as the girl who had disappeared one winter's night going to buy bread at Zabar's. I should have conveyed what I knew to Harry, but, instead, I had decided to approach the revelation of her being alive in my own fashion, which meant after much careful and literary reflection. Dante, my Florentine poet guide, promised no help in this area, since Pinsky's excellent translation was still buried beneath the daybed in our living room, where Harry had kicked it by accident on his way from bedroom to bathroom one drowsy morning. I turned to Proust and his prodigious work on memory but, alas, was asleep before the first madeleine. So I crossed the Channel to the land of Dickens. Dickens mixes his poetry with practicality, and his novels, of course, are stock full of people disappearing and popping up again. I began to work my way through *Great Expectations* in a small-print, nose-unfriendly paperback edition, and as Pip and Estella and Miss Havisham rose up to me from the page and began to play—not very nicely, those last two—in my imagination, I realized, once again, something that I have always known but frequently forget: literature is not a way to get practical things done. Nor should it be. It is a destination and occasionally an escape. When we return to this so-called real world from the book, it is like stepping back into time at the exact moment we had left. We may feel different, but nothing else has changed. And if we are different, we are different in ways that might be rich, wide and soulful, but not really practical. Go into a great novel or poem looking for the answer to A and you'll get the answer to Z. It will be a good answer. But it will still be the answer to Z, not A.

"Harry, we think Imogen is alive," Detective Davis said in a soft voice. He reached out and rested a hand on my owner's shoulder. "We think that she has been living here for several months."

"In this boardinghouse?" Harry asked.

"In this room," Detective Davis said.

Harry looked the tiny space up and down. His eyes came to rest on the queen-sized bed, with its dingy bedspread and its two mauve pillows undisturbed despite the corpse beside them.

"But I thought this was his room?"

"It was his room... and it was her room too."

"They were together?"

Detective Davis nodded.

"A couple?"

"I'm sorry, Harry. They didn't mix much with the people here, but all the inhabitants agreed on that point. They heard things, you know, from behind the door."

"She's alive," Harry said. "Imogen's alive."

Detective Davis was not a man who normally

looked down at the floor in awkward situations, but he did so now.

"Yes. She's alive. That's the good news. The bad news is that they were seen entering the room together tonight and then two people saw her fleeing from this room shortly before the body was discovered."

Again, Harry struggled to digest the information.

"Harry, Imogen is the prime suspect in the murder of the young man beneath that parachute."

INDEED, THE NEWS WAS grim. Very grim. Harry returned to our apartment with four packs of emergency cigarettes crammed into his jacket pockets and a shopping bag filled with enough liquor to stock a weekend party for a drunken English thespian. We would be in for a long night.

My owner was reeling and so was I. Imogen was alive. But who was she exactly? Such strange facts marred the image of my mistress: champagne glasses, one generously marked with thick red lipstick; a photograph of her in party mode, arm draped around a now-dead man with whom she was apparently living while Harry and I endured a yearlong eclipse of her sun; and then the strong possibility (at least, in the eyes of Detective Davis of the NYPD) that Imogen was a murderess. Was she following in Iris, her mother's, homicidal footsteps? Was a bloody gene blooming? Her dog refused to believe this. The surfaces of things can be deceptive. The photograph could be posed. The expression faked. The living arrangement suggestive of other possibilities.

After all, there was that other photograph in the frame. The picture below the one that so disturbed Harry had transmitted a different message to me. This photograph was taken in long-ago, happy days for our family. I was very familiar with it. Imogen had two copies that I knew of: one was still in a frame next to the bed in our apartment, and the other had been on her desk at the Morgan Archives, where she worked. Even if I didn't have a copy close at hand to refresh my memory, I could have recalled all of the elements vividly: the cozy cluster of three figures, the leafy background, the expressions of glee (Imogen), tongue-protruding, damp-snout blankness in the middle (me) and joy (Harry). The photograph had been taken in Central Park on a fine day in May: low humidity, blue skies and squads of tourists wandering about who were more than willing to stop and participate in a "New York moment" by snapping a photograph of two city-dwelling young lovers and their amiable dog. We made a fine trio. It was this photograph that oc-cupied the lower portion of the frame—but with an alteration. I was still there, but Harry was missing.

Whether Imogen or someone else had removed him, I did not know. Nor did I know whether the photograph had been cut or folded over. My owner was deeply distressed, and after his fifth swig and his eighth or ninth emergency cigarette he had revealed this other photograph and had come to the dismal conclusion that this meant Imogen no longer cared about him.

But I surmised that the photograph carried a message of hope. The crucial fact was that Imogen had displayed the photograph in such a prominent place in her new lodgings. Why keep it at all if it meant nothing to her? And though I was featured, it would have been that day that she remembered and the man who had stood beside me in the photo.

The clock on the microwave arrived at three a.m. and found a Labrador squirming in his corner while his profoundly drunk owner stared deep holes into the wall opposite his La-Z-Boy. Harry needed to know what I knew. Things might look bleak now, but I could at least temper some of his darker imaginings. The knowledge would diminish his pain and focus both of us on the next positive step. In the moments prior to the death of Imogen's mother, Iris, by

Grandfather Oswald's World War II–era-Colt .45 (and her subsequent plummet from the window onto the sidewalk below), Iris revealed several items. We already knew that she had killed several people, including Lyell Overton Minskoff-Hardy, literary light and cultural personage, and had been loved blindly by our friend Jackson for decades. But Iris added these points to our understanding: 1) Imogen was her daughter; 2) Imogen was slated to inherit an enormous Australian mining fortune if she survived to thirty and did not go crazy or prove herself homicidal; 3) Iris had confronted her with these two facts on the day that Imogen disappeared; and 4) there was a rugged Australian character tracking Imogen down for some as-yet-unknown purpose. These revelations, coupled with what I had learned from Imogen's journal and my own scent investigations (I had gotten a noseful when I pursued Imogen down the subway stairs), told me that my mistress had not simply moved on. I was certain, as only a dog can be, that Imogen was loyal. If anything, she was protecting us as she saw fit. Harry needed to know this now.

So here I was once again, ready to compose a message out of Alpha-Bits in the early-morning hours. My owner had ceased staring at the wall.

He had let the empty bottle slide to the floor and was now in a deep slumber. A movie ended on the television and an infomercial began. Dangerously tanned men and women with astoundingly white teeth and sculptured limbs held forth on the virtues of a plastic belt that they swore could build a Grecian physique in minutes a day. Yours Truly felt a momentary sense of relief that his girth is permanently clothed in stylish black, then got to work.

A box of Alpha-Bits stood open on the kitchen table. I lifted my paws and hefted myself up until I could snout-swipe it. The box tipped onto the table with a little bang. Harry stirred in the La-Z-Boy but did not wake. The Alpha-Bits box was empty but for four letters: *O-H-N-O*, which summed the situation up only too well.

MORNING BRINGS THE DOCTOR

A DOG IS DIAGNOSED WITH SOMETHING GRAVE

THE MORNING SUN CUT through the living-room window and inched toward my whiskey-benumbed owner and his Labrador, curled at the base of the La-Z-Boy in guardian fashion. When a sliver of sun reached Harry's eyes, they began to twitch and finally to open at glacial pace. Then he groaned a deep cavernous groan that suggested emergence from the profoundest of hibernations. It was a bearish noise—the sound of a large mammal in sluggish agony. I too was feeling less than wonderful. My limbs were heavy, my paws were sore and the gray matter throbbed beneath the skull. We are sensitive creatures, and naturally I thought I was joining my owner's misery with a sympathetic hangover. I had enjoyed none of the mental escape provided by Harry's stash of C_2H_5OH but would now endure all of the morning-after consequences. I could only hope that my owner's inevitable revulsion at the thought of breakfast did not translate into a missed meal for Yours Truly. I steeled myself against the possibility that Harry would forget to find something in our deeply troubled refrigerator to put in my bowl. I needed to communicate what I knew about Imogen before Detective Davis delivered any more bad news. An empty stomach would make this task very difficult.

Then my owner surprised me. He hopped to his feet. He stretched to the ceiling. He stooped to touch his toes. He did twenty jumping jacks and dropped to the floor for twice that many push-ups. When Harry regained his feet, he made an announcement.

"That's it, Randolph," he said. "I'm free. It's over. She's moved on and so have I. It feels good."

This moment of elation was not to last. A second later Harry was back in the La-Z-Boy and, for the second time in my life, had begun to sob. Human psychology certainly eludes my grasp, but I did what I could to comfort and sidled up to him. Soon, though, he was back on his feet and muttering about being late for a doctor's appointment.

Harry disappeared into the bedroom to get changed, passing his still-unfinished portrait of

Imogen in the corner and turning away from it with a pained expression and a scent that suggested a mother lode of sadness. I did not follow him but listened as drawers were opened and slammed shut again in frustration. Per usual, Harry had put off doing the laundry.

"I need clean socks," Harry said, and began to dig through the hamper that stood just inside his bedroom. "You can't go to the doctor's in dirty socks."

No doubt this conviction was the result of some boyhood programming by Harry's solid and practical midwestern mother. But amid the domestic ruin of our bachelor lives, the clean-socks-for-the-doctor mandate was a difficult one to observe. Once Imogen's presence had kept us males in line and compelled us to follow the basic tenets of the Geneva Convention. But without her we often contributed to each other's decline into barbarism. Lightbulbs went unchanged, plates were stacked in the sink and on every inch of kitchen counter, and newspapers were laid out like carpet over the floors to combat spills that had long ago evaporated. In many places, the newspapers were scratched to pieces during my more nervous and worry-heavy pacings. I had seen Harry commence this mad search for clean clothes many times before, and I knew how it would end.

"These aren't too bad," Harry said, and triumphantly emerged with a tartan pair that hadn't been worn since Christmas.

"I don't know why they're even in here," he continued, making reference to the well-known male theory that dirty clothes left long enough in a hamper actually clean themselves. But a second appraisal convinced my owner otherwise and that, where the hamper treatment had failed, the microwave treatment would not. He scrubbed the socks down in the sink, spun them around like the blades of a propeller and then put them in the microwave oven for five minutes on high. The microwave treatment was always a gamble. You could end up with dry socks or a fire condition. It all seemed to depend on where the items of clothing were placed on the revolving tray. Too far on the outside and they would stay damp. Too close to the center and combustion. But this time, my owner got it right. In no time he had slipped on his warm, dry and relatively clean socks and was headed out the door. I am not a pushy dog, but I could not allow the probability of breakfast to head out the door with him. I delivered an imperative whine.

"Of course you can come, Randolph," Harry said, completely misunderstanding me. I would have preferred to collect my thoughts on the sun-warmed floor of our apartment after an ample breakfast. Instead, he clipped the leash to my collar.

"Dr. Huggins loves dogs," he said, and with that we were out the door and making haste through the still-crisp early-spring air. I had heard of Dr. Christopher Huggins on several occasions. The first time was when the good doctor had prescribed extract of hemlock and barley water to aid in treating Harry's insomnia in those first sleepless months after Imogen went missing. If this sounds like a concoction left wisely unemployed by modern medicine, of course it is. Dr. Huggins liked his friends to call him *SparrowHawk* (the name he derived for himself from a hallucinogenic "spirit quest" in some southwestern desert that had not yet been turned into a theme park or gated community). Dr. Huggins was a practitioner of his own brand of alternative medicine, and while my owner resisted calling him by his spirit name, in a particularly unflattering loss of perspective he had once delivered this little chestnut about the good doctor: "He thinks so far outside the box that he'll probably win a Nobel Prize when the

world catches up and realizes how great he is."
His dog doubted this future turn of events and
watched with trepidation as Harry downed
murky potions to alleviate everything from in-
digestion to something called "psychic overload" from his so-called "ghost work" with Ivan
Manners, Harry's friend and a self-styled expert
on the paranormal. Ivan had managed to get
himself showcased on television, and his ghost-
hunting services were now constantly in demand. My owner has played his occasional
apprentice on fruitless expeditions to catch
some evidence of the supernatural with the fly-
paper of technology.

It is not that I am an uncritical fan of
the Western medical tradition or the cult of
the pharmaceutical industry that finds an ail-
ment for every pill, but I didn't think that
SparrowHawk's tinkering would lead to any
miracle cures in Harry, and I was right. I
breathed a sigh of relief when the hemlock
didn't put my owner to sleep like it did Socrates,
that great philosopher and gadfly of Athenian
society. Perhaps Socrates should have mixed his
poison with barley water.

Dr. Huggins operated out of a storefront in
the only dilapidated building on an otherwise
upscale block filled with handbag stores and

tapas restaurants. He shared space with a woman who read palms by appointment and a young man who sold vintage comic books and baseball cards. Neither was there at ten in the morning, but before we had a chance to dawdle on the stoop, the door swung open to reveal Dr. Huggins smoking a pipe filled with ginseng. He wore stained latex gloves sagging at the wrists. But with the exception of the gloves, longish sideburns and a large clay talisman hanging over his pressed oxford, he could have passed for an accountant.

"Harry," Dr. Huggins said. "Welcome, my peer and fellow journeyman."

"Hello, Dr. Huggins," Harry said. "Is it alright if my dog comes in?"

"Is he not a creature of the universe?" Dr. Huggins asked.

Oh Lordy, thought the creature of the universe.

"And please call me SparrowHawk, Harry. It is my true name," Dr. Huggins said as he led us across the threshold, down a hallway lined with questionable diplomas and into a small examination room. Dr. Huggins gestured for Harry to sit on the stainless-steel table. I rested on my haunches in the corner. Dr. Huggins tapped Harry's shoulders with his gloved hands, tweaked my owner's earlobes, touched his index finger to Harry's forehead, sighed and took a step back.

"Wheat allergy," Dr. Huggins announced. "I can see it in your eyes."

Harry massaged his bloodshot, drink-addled eyeballs with his palms.

"It was a rough night," Harry said. The weight of those first hours of wrenching news and horrific revelations about our mistress seemed about to descend again. I detected glistening drops of saline at the corners of his eyes, but my owner fought them back.

"I can see that," Dr. Huggins said. "But what I'm really seeing is deeper than the superficial scrapes of a big night. You, my friend, are definitely allergic to wheat. Why are you here, by the way?"

"We had an appointment," Harry said. "My foot has been hurting."

"I could look at the foot if you want, but your problem begins with wheat," Dr. Huggins said. "You are extremely sensitive to wheat."

"Wheat could affect my foot?" Harry asked.

"Wheat could affect your everything. Your foot. Your libido. Your general sense of happiness and well-being," Dr. Huggins confirmed. "Wheat is one of the worst. As my teacher said about diagnosis, when in doubt, think wheat. It's what we call a *general pernicious* in this biz."

"So what do I do?" Harry asked.

"Avoid wheat at all costs," Dr. Huggins said.

"You mean don't eat it?"

"Don't eat it, don't smell it, don't touch it, don't even look at it."

"I'm that allergic?"

"You're *that* allergic. I could not be more serious," Dr. Huggins averred with a solemn nod.

Then a look of worry, almost desperation, came over my owner.

"Does that include Alpha-Bits?"

"Do they have wheat in them?" asked Dr. Huggins, as if he had never entered a supermarket or watched a television.

"They're cereal."

"Can't eat. Don't eat. Throw out and use gloves with the box. Here's some lavender. It is an essential oil. Dab a little under each nostril before you get home. It counteracts the influence of wheat. Reapply as needed."

I had listened to most of the conversation with amusement, until my owner underscored just what the doctor's instructions would mean. Namely, the part about Alpha-Bits, at which point my amusement turned to deep disturbance. No Alpha-Bits meant that my bridge to Harry—my only avenue to communicate with my owner—was no more. I could only hope that the pure light of reason and good sense would descend once again on my owner, as it had done more regularly in our early days, and he would turn on his heel, walk out of the office and reject all of the nonsense advice. Needless to say, this did not happen.

"Thank you, Dr. Huggins," Harry said.

"It's SparrowHawk to my friends," Dr. Huggins said.

"Right," Harry said, not quite ready to make this leap.

Then Dr. Huggins asked Harry to take off his shoes so that he could examine his foot.

"Nice socks," he pronounced.

"Thanks," Harry said.

"They smell like popcorn."

The doctor twisted Harry's foot and my owner howled in pain.

"Just as I thought; once you stop the wheat, the foot will heal right up."

Harry nodded. Then his gaze turned to me.

"By the way, I know you're not a vet, but could you take a quick look at Randolph? He hasn't been himself lately."

A word on dog health. I am no trained expert,

but I do observe my body and I know what and how I have felt these last five and a half years. I have also communicated with enough of my kind to have a general notion of dog health as opposed to human health. This is my basic conclusion: we dogs don't get sick very much. A cold might annoy the sinuses or irritate the throat. A stomach virus might make our food lose some of its savor. But we soldier on.

That is why, as much as I hated to admit it, Harry was right. Something was wrong with me. I had been under the weather and I wasn't shaking it. I have never had a great deal of zest and have always avoided physical activity, but lately a powerful fatigue was causing me to sleep even longer than my typical Labrador quota and making even minor physical effort almost instantly exhausting. I had even found myself falling asleep over my books, something I had never done before. There were other complaints as well. Since the onset of middle age I have been susceptible to the occasional arthritic ache in the hindquarters on the foggy morning, but this was different—this felt very wrong. Hearing Harry recognize that something might be amiss with his charge was heartening, but realizing that his solution was to entrust me to the questionable

SparrowHawk made me contemplate an escape from the office—if only I had the energy to do it.

Dr. Huggins hefted me onto the examination table with an assist from my owner. Both men paused to catch their breath.

"He's a meaty one," Dr. Huggins panted. "This might be as simple a matter as weight loss."

Dr. Huggins neglected to follow standard hygienic procedures and was now examining me with the same gloves that he had worn for my owner and presumably every other patient who had preceded us. He ran his hand along the top of my snout. I tried to resist, but this dog only has so much willpower, and the effect of a snout rub (even one delivered by a quack wearing dirty gloves) is instantly intoxicating. The tail began to wag.

"You like that, boy," Dr. Huggins cooed in that the-dog-is-naturally-an-idiot voice that humans have reserved especially for us. "Sure, you like that. Good boy."

The glove ran down my back. Patted my generous sides and then—to my horror—attempted entry into Yours Truly's mouth. I resisted, of course, but to no avail. The other glove stunned me with a simultaneous snout rub, and soon my mouth was filled with who knows what kind of bacteria and an ample collection of my own fur.

Then Dr. Huggins turned to Harry.

"I'm not a vet, Harry, but I'd say that your dog has a thyroid condition."

"Oh no."

"I wouldn't worry too much about it. Plenty of Labs have it. It's hypothyroidism. That's what's making him sluggish."

"What do we do?"

For the first time that morning, Dr. Huggins delivered a responsible answer.

"Take him to a vet."

Harry paid the bill, which was something extravagant, thanked the doctor and we set off for home, my owner now limping more distinctly than ever. Harry took SparrowHawk's instructions for his own condition and we stopped at the Duane Reade on the corner of 90th and Columbus. He tied me to a fireplug (no doubt on the theory that no dognapper would want or could lift me) and disappeared inside. A few minutes later he emerged with a bag filled with cleaning supplies, rubber gloves and a face mask for the antiwheat crusade, along with a bulk supply of ginkgo biloba that must have required a whole virgin Amazon forest to produce.

"Ginkgo's good for the brain," Harry declared as he plunked his purchases down on the kitchen table that was soon to be rid of all traces of our favorite breakfast cereal.

Yes, I reflected, *we would be needing brain, and plenty of it.*

CLEANING OF ANY SORT IS a rare event in our apartment. I was not even sure if Harry would know what to do. But he threw himself into the work, and soon the place was mopped, scrubbed, deluged and purified of all traces of wheat and every other delightful, comforting, memory-evoking smell that had made this dog's nose at home. I have spoken of the profound power of the canine olfactories before, but I will mention it again here. Try to imagine if your nose was 100,000 times more powerful than it is. You would live in an utterly different reality. What is now a whiff that brings back a memory would seem to become the memory and assume all its comforting or discomforting dimensions. If you have noticed that I describe much of the action around me in terms of visual gestures, scenes and words—well, that is for your benefit, a kind of translation for the nose-deprived. My dog's eyes are surprisingly good, but my nose is like a psychologist and a lie detector. It is also the organ that orients me most in this world, and so when the carnage of cleaning fluids was over and Harry brought out the vacuum cleaner to finish the job, I retreated to the bedroom, looking for some trace of our former life, some trace of Imogen and lazy Sunday afternoons. I found it beneath the clothes dresser: a small tumbleweed of my fur and several years' accumulation of dust woven into it. I kept it close to my nose until Harry arrived and shooed me away and finally that memory too had vanished up the hose and into the vacuum's stomach.

Harry put the vacuum cleaner away and switched on the television, and Yours Truly curled up in the corner beneath the easel with the unfinished painting of Imogen and nursed his spinning brain.

Then the telephone rang and my disorientation grew worse. It was Zest Kilpatrick. This overly energized local-television news reporter had met my owner at the Pooch Palace a few months earlier and tried to force her way onto Harry's social calendar. This attempt failed despite the fact that my owner's social calendar was empty. They had not exchanged phone numbers, but she had left us with her business card. The telephone call proceeded as follows (Zest spoke so loudly that both sides of the conversation were quite audible):

"Harry," Zest said.

"Yes."

"This is Zest."

"Zest?"

"Zest Kilpatrick. Channel Eight. News on the Eight. I know this is forward but Ivan Manners suggested it. You know how involved he and Mr. Apples are with the bird cause. I'd like to invite you to come to the Lorikeet Rescue Fund annual dinner at the Discovery Society three days from now. I know it's short notice, but I figured, what the hell, he's cute. Ha-ha. I'm such an idiot. I did *not* just mean to say that. So what do you think? Can you make it? It's fine to say no. I understand. No pressure. Say no if you want."

"Yes," Harry said. "I'd like to come."

"I mean, it's for the birds," Zest said. "That doesn't sound right. I mean it's for a good cause. The birds."

"I understand," Harry said. "It would be fun. I'd like to see you."

The phone call concluded and this dog's brain reeled. Going to a dinner at which Ivan Manners and Mr. Apples, his Farsi-speaking rainbow lorikeet, were present was grim enough. But my owner's behavior was even more unwelcome. Savaging our apartment with the scent-wasting vacuum was minor compared to this gesture of openness to another woman, particularly *this* overly anxious, clock-ticking predator. The assessment was likely unfair, but I believed that Harry's loyalties lay with Imogen, no matter what he might have said that morning. For him to look elsewhere was a kind of desecration.

But I did not have long to contemplate this betrayal when the buzzer rang. It was Detective Davis. He was carrying a small shopping bag and wore a grim expression.

"Harry," Detective Davis said as he came into the apartment.

"Peter," Harry answered.

"What's wrong with your leg?"

"Wheat," Harry said.

Detective Davis shrugged. He had once been a Buddhist monk, and this training, combined with his tenure as a New York City police detective, had apparently given him the ability to hear the most absurd nonsense without betraying the slightest surprise.

"Wheat," he echoed. "I didn't know wheat could do that to you."

"I have an allergy," Harry explained. "Do you want to sit down?"

Detective Davis looked at his limited options and shook his head.

"Things are developing very fast, Harry. Imogen's DNA is all over that room and all over that parachute cord."

"You actually think she could have killed him?" Harry asked. "I can't believe it."

"I can't believe it either, Harry," Detective Davis said. "But she's in the crosshairs. There is one very puzzling detail, though. Remember I told you that the victim was probably drugged and we'd find evidence of that in the champagne glass?"

"Yes."

"Well, we did. He was drugged—toxicology showed us that overnight—but both champagne glasses have heavy traces of the drug chloral hydrate. Not just his glass; her DNA is all over the other glass. We have every reason to believe that she consumed it too. Not to be too clinical, but her saliva was in the champagne."

"Maybe she only had a sip."

Detective Davis shook his head.

"A sip would put a gorilla down. There's something else too. The dead man was a foreign national. He worked at the United Nations as a sous-chef in their international dining room."

"Oh?" Harry asked.

"He had several names and several passports. We don't even know what nationality he is. At the risk of sounding dramatic: there are bigger forces at work here. Maybe global forces. Imogen didn't disappear for nothing the first time, and she's running from more than just the NYPD now."

"You mean what Iris said could be true?" Harry asked. "That Imogen had some kind of fortune coming to her?"

"I can't say," Detective Davis said.

"But that story couldn't have been true. She was born in Akron, Ohio. She went to live with her grandmother in Kentucky after her parents divorced."

"Harry, Imogen wasn't born in Akron and she never attended school in Kentucky."

"But she went to Amherst."

"Yes, she did," Detective Davis said. "And their records show that she spent high school in Austria."

"How long have you known this?"

"Since this morning."

"I mean, shouldn't we have known this when she went missing the first time?"

"We should have," Detective Davis said. "But we didn't because, unbeknownst to me, one of my guys relied on computer records. This time I called Amherst myself and they went to the hard archives."

"Why were the computer records wrong?"

"I don't know."

Harry stared at the floor.

"So she's someone else," my owner muttered.

"I don't know about that," Detective Davis said. "She hid some things from you."

"Some things?" Harry said. "She hid her life."

"There's a lot that we don't know, Harry," Detective Davis said. "The fact that the victim's trail leads to the United Nations dining room makes things complicated. NYPD has to tread delicately in diplomatic circles. We can't push things. Already I'm getting resistance."

"This doesn't involve me anymore, does it?" Harry said. "Imogen's gone and she didn't want to take me with her. If she was in trouble, she could have told me."

"I can't speak to that, Harry," Detective Davis answered. "I've seen people disappear for the stupidest reasons. But it does involve you. If she contacts you, you need to contact me immediately."

"Why would she?" Harry said.

"*If* she does. It's guilty until proven innocent in this country, but you don't want to risk being seen as an accessory."

"Right," Harry said. "I'll call you. What's in the bag?"

"A little something for Randolph. Liverwurst," Detective Davis said. "My dogs used to go crazy for liverwurst."

PORK. PORK LIVER. COOKED
goose. Goose fat. Goose liver. Salt.

These were the first six ingredi-
ents listed on the golden package that Detective
Davis left with my owner for me. When Davis
left, Harry tossed the liverwurst onto the floor,
unopened, and sank into the La-Z-Boy.

"All yours, boy," Harry said. "Come and
get it."

My head still spun from the loss of our apartment's familiar scents and the added burden of
Detective Davis's revelations about Imogen, but
a Lab's stomach is a powerful force and I was
drawn to this new foodstuff. I had never encountered liverwurst before. It is a German delicacy
seldom found on a dog's plate. I hesitate to admit
even to myself what a slave I am to my lower natures. How even as I cringe at the antics of my
kind at the dog run—the hindquarter sniffing,
the indiscriminate urination, et cetera—I under-

stand it all too well. And sometimes, restrained *Foliage-Finder* though I am, scent and the demands of the stomach can unite to overpower me. Such was the near-mystical power of the small golden package of liverwurst that rolled to a stop right beneath my nose.

In a blur of torn plastic casing, I soon found myself with large gobs of the stuff all over my mouth and stuck to my paws and snout. The smell was rich and transcendent. I believe I rolled across the floor. Possibly several times. Undoubtedly the tail was up to its wagging—this time completely justified—as the jaws chomped and the tongue moved and the throat swallowed the ambrosia down. To be a dog at times like this is to be perfectly in sync with some fundamental universal principle. It is to have found the key to life. From a hazy distance I heard Harry make some comment and then the package was being yanked away.

"Randolph," Harry said. "You can't eat the whole thing. Show some restraint. It's embarrassing."

As far as wolf-pack dynamics go, Imogen was my alpha figure, but Harry has some kind of alpha status and so his scolding cuts deep. The tail froze and sank, as did my head. The eyes looked up. I believe I even cowered.

"No, Randolph, it's my fault," Harry said. "How can I expect an animal to show restraint?"

I shook off the hereditary shame response and gave a loud snuffle, which does wonders to expel bad humor.

"At least we know another food that you like. Not that there's a limited number," Harry said. He took the remaining liverwurst, wrapped it in a scrap of aluminum foil he found under the sink and deposited it in our still deeply troubled refrigerator (Harry's cleaning binge had come to a dead stop before this wilderness). My eyes followed the disappearing golden package like it was a sacred relic.

"Now what are we going to do?" Harry asked. As the liverwurst-induced fog began to recede, I could sense that Harry was in a place he had not been in before. He was still forlorn, as he had been for so many months in the absence of Imogen, but now there was a kind of resolve building. It was the kind of resolve that appears after disillusionment. In other words, it was the wrong kind of resolve. It was a hardening. It was a rejection. It was a loss of faith. In an instant, I felt ashamed for a reason far beyond my little liverwurst bacchanalia. How could I have failed both of them so badly? Why had I hesitated to communicate to Harry what I knew about

Imogen when I had the power to do so? Now what could I do? The Alpha-Bits were gone. There was no bridge between species and no way for me to let him know that I believed Imogen had likely disappeared to protect us. And then, in a turn of events that frequently happens in novels but rarely in real life, my owner provided the answer: he decided to dust off his laptop computer and connect to the Internet.

The computer had been stowed on the bookcase since Imogen disappeared. One might have thought that Harry—desperate to hear some word from her—would never have put the computer away in the first place, but Harry and Imogen were a peculiar couple. They were technology-wary. They did not own cell phones, for example, and the laptop had been given to Harry by the midwestern patriarch, concerned that his son was falling behind the technology curve. Harry and Imogen had steered clear of e-mail, and all of their text-messaging was done with pen and paper. It was just their way.

"I've been out of the loop so long that I'm not even sure where the loop is," Harry announced, hitting the false I'm-an-old-fogy note as he flipped open the screen and powered up the device. "I'll see if I can get online."

Online... The word echoed with an almost mythic potential, like F. Scott Fitzgerald's *fresh, green breast of the new world*. I had read about the Internet with fascination, but as a lover of books and contemplation I still had my reservations. What did such instant communication and connection mean? Was being *online* something that would defeat the inborn reflectivness of the reader and thinker? Did *high speed* equal shallow, hasty and empty? Even so, the moment that Harry mentioned it, I saw a path out of the present incommunicative dilemma.

I sidled up to my owner and received a pat on the head while the laptop searched the vicinity for a connection. Fortunately, many of our neighbors had unsecured networks, and my owner was soon piggybacking on someone else's connection. These terms meant nothing to me, but I gathered the proper nomenclature from my owner's mutterings. I further learned that his e-mail account had long ago lapsed and that he was now opening a new one. I thought the address might come in handy and made a mental note of the ungainly and faintly embarrassing moniker: *Harryghostpainter2* (apparently *Harryghostpainter1* had already been taken).

Having set up an e-mail account, Harry commenced to surf. I rested my chin on the arm of the La-Z-Boy and soon was entranced by what I saw on the screen. The flowing virtual geometries of cyberspace, the images and the words, the many different fonts and shades: it was like television, but the viewer was at least partially in control. I watched Harry navigate from one page to the next. The word *navigate* itself evoked the heady possibilities of a journey across wide oceans. *Surf, navigate, wide oceans*... freedom. A world beyond the tyranny of the leash.

The first obstacle would be finding enough time alone with the machine to learn how to use it. I could only hope that Harry would leave the laptop open and accessible. Alpha-Bits had been snout-challenging, but the tiny keys of Harry's computer and the cursor-manipulating "touch" pad would demand still-untapped reserves in Yours Truly. Yes, there would be profound neck strain and nose angst in my near future. But even my newly diagnosed medical condition would not stop me from supplying my owner with the truth. Speaking of which, Harry, betraying uncharacteristic efficiency, scheduled an appointment online for Yours Truly that very day at our local veterinary office. A small victory for responsible pet ownership.

Harry then found his way to Ivan Manners's site, which featured the rotund exhibitionist urging all visitors to respect the paranormal, use his ghost-hunting services and contribute to the Lorikeet Rescue Fund. But before my owner could linger there, the surf of the nonvirtual world broke over us in the shape of a phone call and swept us in an entirely new direction. It was Jackson Temple, Harry's friend and benefactor. He wanted to meet both of us in Midtown right away.

HARRY PLACED THE LAP-
top on the kitchen table and picked
his jacket off the floor.

"Well, Randolph, this should be interesting,"
Harry sounded a dubious note. Jackson, after
all, seldom saw us anywhere but in his cluttered
suite at the Belvedere Hotel, where he had lived
for decades among teetering stacks of books
and the objets d'art of an eccentric collector.
He was an independently wealthy man who was
a well-regarded art historian. As I have mentioned, Jackson had loved Iris. He had also
watched her die in that tense scene less than a
month before. But he was a philosophical man
and well bred—whatever pain he felt seldom
reached the surface to mar his good manners.
There was never any question of despising
Harry because he had shot Iris before she finished the job by plummeting to the sidewalk.
Jackson, it seemed, understood and forgave, if

there was anything to forgive. But the call was strange, because Jackson wasn't spontaneous. A visit usually had some reason.

Harry hurried me along the sidewalk, rushing me through a thicket of scents. My nose brushed flower-bed rails and verdant sidewalk cracks. Spring was coming fast. It was pushing up through the thick stone crust that covered Manhattan's living earth, and it was in the air billowing down from the nascent buds and the temperate sky. I breathed it all deeply and let my four legs resist Harry's forward pull. But then we reached the curb and I looked up to see my owner hailing a taxi. New York taxis seldom take big dogs—I don't think they're allowed unless my kind is caged. But try enough times to convince someone to go along with almost anything in Manhattan and you'll succeed. After the fifth taxi had screamed by, an SUV hybrid decided to take a chance, and in fifteen minutes we found ourselves stepping out across the street from the United Nations. Midtown Manhattan is so much larger and more monumental than the Upper West Side. The coziness of our domain, with its narrow streets and residential buildings, seems far distant from the steel and glass austerities of consulates, corporations and NGOs—the workaday world of diplomats, businessmen and activists—but, in fact, our home is only a few miles distant. Even so, I had never seen the United Nations outside of photographs, and I was moved by the swooping roof of the main building and the general serenity of the place. At the same time I noticed how tired things looked. The tower—a modern wonder in its day—appeared worn and dated, its windows stained, unmatched and even peeling in places. It was as if I were looking at the visible evidence of the cost of humans trying to get along with one another. Harry interrupted these silent elegies with a brusque leash tug.

"Randolph, get out of the street," he commanded. This was followed by the blare of several taxis navigating around my hindquarters at dangerous speeds. Jackson waited on the sidewalk.

"It's good to see you," Jackson said, giving Harry a strong handshake. "You look good, but Mister Randolph seems a bit out of it."

"Mister Randolph has just been diagnosed with hypothyroidism," Harry said. "That's when the thyroid—"

"Doesn't produce enough thyroxine, I know," Jackson finished.

"How?"

"It's a common condition in Labs *and*

Guatemalan tree sloths, except in Guatemalan tree sloths it's essentially normal. If you treat it, you turn your sloth into a Hunter S. Thompson with fur—all wired for sound," Jackson said. Jackson knew of such things because he was the owner of Marlin, a sloth and a fine fellow, whose body traveled in laborious inches about his tree but whose mind moved with whip-smart speed.

"Come with me," Jackson said. He turned and led the way into a narrow building whose façade was clear blue glass. The ceiling of the lobby was high above us, and a large mobile composed of dangling hubcaps and tire irons was pushed in circles by a gentle current. The floor and the reception desk, behind which an ancient guard drowsed, were black marble polished to an astonishing shine.

"Austere but majestic," Jackson suggested.

"Where are we?"

"WAHA," Jackson said. "The World Artistic Heritage Association. It's a group of wealty duffers and starry-eyed Don Quixotes dedicated to the preservation of the visual arts and the community of world artists. I'm on the board. Our staff does good work when they're not at the pub frittering our money away on grog and loose women."

"That's a joke."

"Not really, I'm afraid."

As if on cue, the elevator door—polished to a gemlike shine—opened to disgorge what looked like a drunken elf smoking a pipe the size of a small croquet mallet.

"An artist?" Harry asked under his breath as the man hurried by without a glance at any of us.

"An administrative assistant. He manages the database," Jackson corrected. "Needless to say, the place does not run like a well-oiled machine. But at least it has character and spirit. Yes, lots of character and spirit."

Jackson gestured at the far wall between the two elevators.

"Something this place doesn't have is art. Not a scrap, unless you call that circling junkyard above our heads art. It's difficult, of course, to fit any art in, with all of this steel, glass and stone. The architect made sure of that. He didn't want anything to spoil his vision—you know, they've all tried to get away with the same nonsense since Frank Lloyd Wright. I understand it—they're making art too, and artists like absolute control—but there has to be a limit. In the end we battled the man back and we got that space with which we can do as we please. Thirty feet by ten feet, and we want a mosaic. And I want *you* to do it for us. Harry, this is the commission I spoke about at Christmas. Are you ready for it now?"

"A mosaic?" Harry asked. "Of what?"

"A mosaic that depicts WAHA's mission."

"But I haven't had much experience with mosaics."

"I believe in you. Besides, anything would be better than that goddamn mobile."

"Jackson, I'm honored. This is a big project," Harry said.

"It's a career-maker, Harry. If you do it right," Jackson said, "it could be a major work."

"I don't know."

"Think it over if you want, but I've managed to convince the board that you're the man for the job, even though there are others in line to do the work. Your résumé could use it; you're all bits and pieces right now—superbly done but nothing cohesive. I want something special on that wall. I want something that carries people walking through that door well beyond what they are used to. I want art—real art—the kind of work they say no one can do anymore because we're over it all, because we've moved on, grown cynical, don't or can't believe in anything. But I don't accept that view. Things are cyclical. Culture gets a body blow and shudders, and for fifty years no one can produce anything but

crap; then the cultural body starts healing and
we've got good work being done again. And
good work is the kind of work you are capable of
doing. I know that. I've supported you because
of that—I like you too, Harry, you're a good guy,
but you're an even better artist, and it's time
that you started doing something about it. You
know I'm usually not this emphatic—it's not a
comfortable mode—but I can see the need in
your face. You're at a critical juncture. There's
either change in your life or hardening into
something that can't change."

"There's news about Imogen," Harry said,
and stared down at the floor. "Bad news."

"I'm sorry to hear that," Jackson said. I expected Jackson to stop and try to comfort my
owner, but instead he became more strident.
"But at the risk of sounding harsh and uncaring,
whatever the news is, that wall is waiting. You
have that gift of yours and you have that wall.
No woman—especially not Imogen—would ever
want you to stop that gift. No woman worth anything would stop you from spending your wak-
ing, working life doing exactly what you were
meant to be doing. Bad news or good news can
disrupt you, but it mustn't derail you."

I could tell my owner was stunned by
Jackson's words. His benefactor and friend had

never delivered anything but consolation where Imogen was concerned. For a moment I thought Harry would snap, but he didn't.

"I'll do it," he said. "I'd love to do it. You're right. It's time to move on."

"I hope you know I'm not saying this because of my disillusionment with Iris," Jackson said. "I'm not starting a chapter of the He-Man-Woman-Haters' Club, but whatever happens with Imogen, it is time to start working again."

"I know. I will," Harry said. "They think Imogen's alive."

"Thank God," Jackson said. "I admit to thinking the worst when Iris said that she had seen her on the day she disappeared."

It was Jackson's turn to fall silent.

"It's still painful, isn't it?" Harry asked.

"Yes," Jackson said. "It shouldn't be, but it is. We humans are a strange breed. We love all the wrong things."

"So what's involved?" Harry asked.

"This is something of an extraordinary commission in that there will be no oversight. You are free to create as you see fit. There is a budget, but it is flexible. There are only two requirements, but they're significant: one, whatever ends up on that wall must have something to reflect the essence of WAHA's mission—the notion of preservation and promotion of world art—and, two, you must show up for work every day, five days a week, until the work is done."

"I can do that, but the second condition is a little weird," Harry said.

"It's my requirement," Jackson said. "I think it's the best thing for you. There'll be days that you doubt doing this. There'll be days that you want to head back to the La-Z-Boy and stay there for the rest of your life, but you won't because you have to be somewhere—you'll have to be here. Because if you aren't—even if it's just one day—you lose the commission and, as much as it pains me, you're going to lose my support too."

Once again I thought Harry would balk at Jackson. Harry is a quiet young man, but he is not the type of person to be pushed around. It was only a few months before that he had charged off to work at the mere reminder that Jackson paid our bills.

"I understand," Harry said. "Thank you."

"I hoped you'd take it that way," Jackson said.

"So when do I start?"

"Tomorrow," Jackson said. "Now, if you come with me, I want to show you one of the perks of the job."

Jackson nodded at the ancient guard, who

still dozed behind the black marble monolith that was reception despite Jackson's rousing speech that had rallied our promising young artist.

"WAHA's what they call a 'relaxed work environment,'" Jackson observed as he led the way down a corridor to a pair of double doors. "All of the administrative offices are upstairs and, if you're lucky, you'll never have to go up there."

"The domain of that tiny drunk man," Harry said.

"Yes, among others. Incredible the oddities that roll through the doors of a nonprofit and find permanent employment. As I said, if you're lucky you'll never have to go up there."

Jackson pushed both doors open in dramatic fashion to reveal a huge storage room with unfinished concrete-block walls, rows of fluorescent lights on the ceiling and a playing field of floor space.

"This will be your workshop. You can order any machines and supplies that you think you might need and keep them here. It isn't much…"

"I could build the Statue of Liberty in here," Harry said. "It's enormous."

My owner walked over to an object in the middle of the room. It was covered by a bright red tarp.

"What's this?"

"That is the perk," Jackson said, and smiled. "Take off the tarp."

Harry pulled at the covering and it dropped in a heap on the floor.

WHAT LAY BENEATH THE sheet was an object that has been labeled by others more knowledgeable than Yours Truly as the epitome of Italian design. It was a Vespa—specifically, a 150cc PX model with a Granturismo frame and large twelve-inch wheels. Harry instantly appreciated the device beneath the tarp.

"Beautiful," he pronounced.

A Vespa is indeed a beautiful machine. It was designed by an aeronautical engineer, Corradino D'Ascanio, who hated motorcycles and had been recruited in 1946 to create a scooter that would be revolutionary. It needed to carry both men and women, to carry a passenger and to protect anyone on board from the dirt and water of the road. The result was a vehicle that looked like a sculpture but could reach speeds in excess of eighty-five mph. The engine was mounted on the rear wheel, and the scooter

featured a "pass-through leg area" so women
wearing skirts and dresses could ride without
inconvenience or embarrassment (apparently
very important in Bella Italia). Yes, the vehicle
was a triumph of engineering and design, but
it also helped that popular culture was on its
side—in the form of Audrey Hepburn and
Gregory Peck speeding through *Roman Holiday*
on the back of a Vespa. They were followed by
legions of celebrities and fictional characters,
including John Wayne and Salvador Dali (whose
"surrealized" Vespa is now in a museum). The
Mod youth of 1960s Britain made the Vespa a
fixture of that country's roadways, but despite
John Wayne's appreciation of the machine, it
never caught on in the United States. The heavy
rain and snow of the Northeast might explain
why Vespa ridership was never particularly high
in Manhattan, but a better reason was probably
the soundness of our public transportation system and the fact that rushing on a small scooter
through streets filled with drivers from every
corner of the globe, each piloting large, carnivo-
rous American vehicles, seemed unappealing to
all but the most rugged. Of course, New York
was changing—a new current of civility had
swept across the cityscape with the turn of the

century. In this gentler place, the artistic Vespa almost looked survivable.

"It's mine?" Harry asked.

"It's yours for the duration of the project," Jackson said. "I thought it would make sense. It'll get you here faster, especially with your foot. What's wrong, by the way—that's quite a bad limp."

"It's my wheat allergy," Harry said, sounding unconvinced himself, as he hobbled around the vehicle like a child surveying an astounding gift. "I'm happy it's silver. I've seen them in pink."

"And it's been adapted for your companion," Jackson said. With a sinking of the stomach and a weakness in the paws, I realized that Jackson meant me. "The seat behind the driver has been widened for Randolph, and there's a way to lock him in so he doesn't take a nasty tumble into the middle of Broadway or some such."

Indeed, the backseat had been amply widened and possessed padded sides that swung into place to create a sort of box where I was to sit.

Harry, who had knowledge of dogs riding aboard two-wheeled vehicles from his midwestern experience, admired the design but questioned the necessity.

"I've seen farm dogs ride on the back of

much narrower bikes, no problem," my owner said. "But, then again, we're speaking about Randolph."

"I doubt if a farm dog could stay on for long in a contest with a New York City pothole, or look sophisticated doing it," Jackson said.

I was about to snuffle in support but thought better of it lest I was understood. Once in puppyhood, the spareribs and plum sauce had arrived with a fortune cookie whose message I read and still value: *To be underestimated is to remain free.*

"Well, my boy, I have a lunch of academics to attend. Pray for me—there is nothing more frightening than sitting in a room filled with people who have tenure and know it."

"What about the bike?" Harry asked.

"By all means, ride it home," Jackson said.

"But I don't see a license plate," Harry muttered.

"That's the beauty of the thing. Check the storage compartment," Jackson said.

Harry lifted the seat and pulled out a small license plate.

"The license plate is on Velcro, so when you park on the sidewalk in front of your apartment—which I have been told is brazenly illegal—you simply remove the license plate from the back of the Vespa, stow it in the storage compartment and the ticketing authorities will be unable to issue a summons."

"Clever," Harry said.

"It was the elf's idea. He's very savvy when it comes to these things."

"So you think it's fine to break the law?"

"It's the spirit of the thing that matters," Jackson said. "With all this talk about fossil fuels and making New York air as fresh as a mountain glade, I suspect they'll welcome one more young man and his dog speeding about town on such a vehicle. Besides, if it gets towed, we'll let WAHA worry about it."

Then Jackson turned and fixed Harry with his eyes.

"I'm really very happy that you've agreed to do this, Harry. It is a very good thing indeed."

Harry looked mildly embarrassed, and Jackson passed through the double doors with a wave of his hand. Silence rushed in when his footsteps had finally disappeared and my owner and I were left alone to commune with the glistening machine. There is something about a new vehicle that can defeat (at least temporarily) the glummest of moods. I have spoken of the power of my dog's nose before and how even emotion and mental states are within its reach.

Harry was exuberant. I had not smelled exuberance in our house for a very long time. Its scent falls somewhere between a fine piece of steak grilling on a open flame for a summer barbecue and gunpowder. My owner might have been more of a motorcycle than a Vespa type, but he had had precious little experience with either. The smell, in this case, was closer to gunpowder.

"Well, Randolph," he said. "It looks like we've got a new ride. I guess I should practice, but how hard could it be? It's just a bicycle with a motor. Come on, let's go."

Harry pushed the vehicle out the double doors, through the lobby and past the ancient guard, who was still fast asleep.

When we were curbside, my owner rummaged through the storage compartment until he emerged with a helmet for himself. There would be no head protection for the dog's gray matter. Then he looked down at me.

My stomach shuddered once again and I instinctively dropped to the pavement.

"Oh no you don't, you big coward," Harry said. "You're riding in the back if I have to tie you there."

My owner reached down and heaved me up onto the seat. Then he raised the side panels and clicked them into place one by one.

"Now, how do you start this thing?" Harry asked as he slid into place in front of me. His dog only stared off to the side and tried to ignore the stream of fast-moving traffic speeding up First Avenue a dozen or so yards in front of us—a five-lane current that would soon digest us. Harry searched for a motorcycle kick-starter with his foot but could find none—one of the things D'Ascanio hated about motorcycles was the kick-starter, so no Vespa ever had one. After several minutes of this, a passing man dressed in an expensive-looking suit noticed Harry's problem and stopped. He addressed my owner in perfect English, with only the hint of an Italian accent, and explained that the Vespa was activated by a key, which he went on to point out was already conveniently located in the ignition.

"A real diplomat," Harry grumbled, as the man walked off in the direction of the United Nations. The machine hummed to life. The lack of a roar momentarily comforted me, but little did either of us know that we were aboard the GT250ie version equipped with the new QUASAR system (Quarter-liter Smooth Augmented Range). The fuel injection meant that our craft was capable of Labrador-unfriendly speeds. This fact was discovered when we squealed onto First Avenue in a miasma of burning rubber and jamming brakes.

"Now we're cooking with gas," Harry observed with unnecessary bravado as he wedged us between an uptown bus and a car ringed with purple lights and throbbing like a discotheque. By 60th Street, my central processing unit had failed before the vision of two or three near misses and an altercation with a bicycle messenger, who struck out at Harry's disappearing head (and his dog's most vulnerable back) with a cardboard tube marked *Priority—Architectural—The Children's Hospital.* I buried my nose in Harry's jacket and searched for some familiar scents that would ground me and help me regain my composure. But as we crossed 70th, my attitude changed. Our continued survival seemed likely, my owner had begun to tame the machine and drive sensibly and I recognized that there was a rich treasure of scents streaming past me—all of Manhattan was in the air. I straightened up and rested my chin on Harry's shoulder. Great gusts of New York City's essence streamed into my nostrils. Bagels and hot dogs. Falafels and Tastee Delite. Chinese and Indian. Tibetan and Italian. Ethiopian and McDonald's. The new life of budding trees and flowers mingled with the decay of restaurant refuse and gutter grit. This was heady stuff, well beyond the possibilities of a cracked window in a car. The scents, the rush of air, the speed, seemed to heighten my senses and freeze the city into a kind of *tableau vivant*—a living photograph, a fantastic spectacle of isolated images speeding toward me like a kaleidoscopic fantasy that liberated individuals from the collective blur. If New York is anything, it is its endless parade of characters. A man clomped along the sidewalk in a diving mask and a snorkel. Another man, in a linen suit with a shoestring tie, held aloft a book entitled *The Power of the Now*. He seemed about to proclaim something to an audience of turned backs and lowered heads. A young mother stared wonderstruck into the carriage she was pushing, as if she had just discovered Einstein's Unified Field Theory tangled among the blankets and plush toys instead of her baby. A traffic policeman waved her white gloves and, ignored by all, finally decided to light a cigarette.

"Having a good time, boy?" Harry shouted above the racing air. *Yes,* I would have replied, *a good time is one way of putting this transcendence.*

Then the light changed and we came to a stop. A well-groomed woman crossed the street in front of us, clutching a tiny animal to her chest with one hand and holding an expensive-looking handbag in the other. The animal appeared to be some kind of dog, but I could not immediately pick the breed. It was ungainly, out of proportion, awkward. If it had been walking on its own instead of being carried like a handbag, it would have galumphed. Then I realized—in a moment of horror tempered by amusement—that I was looking at a walking oxymoron. I had heard rumors of this breed but had dismissed them as mere myth. But, indeed, right before my eyes was proof. It was a miniature Great Dane, the bonsai tree of canines. The *Walk* signal vanished and the *Don't Walk* signal began to flash. But the woman did not hurry, and just as she passed in front of us, the little fellow gave me a mournful look.

Naturally I was abashed and would have promptly apologized for staring, but the light changed. Harry once again set our GT250ie into furious motion up the avenue, before making a sudden turn onto 97th for the trip across the park.

There would soon be the smell of trees and acres of green earth filling the air, but the speedball effect had fled. I felt a sudden heaviness come over me. SparrowHawk would have ascribed it to the hypothyroidism. But I was certain that it came from my distinct sense of guilt and failure. Even the most sophisticated and intelligent dog wants to please his human for reasons utterly beyond the scope of the conscious mind. Primitive reasons they may be, but noble as well.

A young man was dead beneath a parachute. My mistress was a suspect and my owner was speeding away from her and the grief that kept them whole—and I was frolicking. I curled into a tight ball and sank low in my passenger basket, feeling every bump of the road.

Then, as if Yours Truly's mood could not become blacker, Harry muttered a name that brought back the blackest of my puppy memories: *Haddy McClay.*

Rising to my feet, I saw that we had reached our street and idling in front of our building was a familiar convertible, which, despite the early-spring chill, had its top down.

THE IDLING CONVERTible contained Harry's sister, Iberia, his brother-in-law, a Scottish banker named Tony, and their daughter, Haddy McClay. This eight-year-old child was the reason for the creeping nerve tingle that had turned each follicle of hair on my back into ice. The reader will likely recognize how my kind is usually tentative, even skittish, around children. Part of this is because on some primitive pack level we identify the so-called top dogs instantly, and children are never top dogs. The most forceful child still lacks natural authority. But there is another, more pressing reason: we don't trust the little blighters. Even when their adults are watching them, they don't hesitate to rough us up. Our tails seem to fascinate them, possibly on the theory that they are detachable. They also yank our legs, squeeze our noses and pull our ears. They try to make us walk on two legs or sit in chairs. They wrap napkins around our heads and jam sunglasses over our eyes. One dog of my acquaintance was imprisoned in a hammock. Another painted purple to look like a grape. And when we don't play with them and scurry, tail at half mast, into the next room, then they complain to their elders and stern words are issued in our direction. I don't mean to sound uncharitable, but try, if you dare, to go through your day without your dynamic human hands and arms to defend yourself, and you will know of what I speak.

Fortunately, Haddy McClay and her family lived deep in the moneyed woods and manicured gardens of Fairfield County and led one of those hectic, self-absorbed modern lives that meant we rarely saw them. In fact, my deep fear and distrust of this little girl stemmed from a single visit one Christmas several years earlier when she fed me a box of saltines and I unwittingly ate them—not realizing that the diabolical child had also hidden my water bowl in the cabinet beneath the sink. Eventually, after an agonizing hour of resistance—and beaten down by a profound Saharan thirst—I succumbed, and she gleefully watched as Yours Truly plunged his head into the toilet bowl for a long drink.

"Harry, how *are* you, little brother?" Iberia said. The tight bun of his sister's high-strung hairdo whipped around in our direction and revealed the eyes of a suburban gladiator. Harry and Iberia were separated in age by only a few years, but they were generations and temperaments apart. Where Harry is gentle, considerate and slow-moving, Iberia is harsh, heedless of others and seldom at rest. She is also astoundingly selfish. The world, I suspect, is divided into those who take and those who give. Iberia was one of the former; Harry, one of the latter. And if you are the one who gives, you can never stay around someone who takes for very long or soon there will be nothing of yourself left. Harry had learned this lesson young with Iberia. Iberia had gone to California for college. Harry had gone in the opposite direction, arrived in Manhattan and never left. Even though Iberia married and settled within an hour of New York, our little island's natural defenses managed to keep her at bay. Imogen's presence had also helped (Iberia thought my mistress was aloof), but even after Imogen's disappearance and a perfunctory show of support in those first few terrible weeks, Iberia had stayed away. Until now. Now she was here to take, I thought. But I was wrong (at least technically). Iberia wasn't taking; she was giving Harry her daughter to look after while she and Tony jetted off to Paradise Island for a banking conference. For a week. And then another week while they went to a private resort on the Exumas for a "real" holiday.

"Haddy won't be any trouble, I swear," Iberia said as disbelief spread across her brother's face. I wondered which was more incredible: that Iberia had the temerity to appear on our doorstep and make such a request or that she actually believed that my unemployed, lovelorn, bohemian owner was capable of keeping her child in one piece for two weeks. Then again, I mused, perhaps she didn't care.

"Sorry for the short notice. Didn't you get my e-mail?"

"I don't have e-mail. Well, I didn't until this morning," Harry muttered. "I have a phone."

"Never mind. It doesn't matter now. You've got to stay in the loop, little brother. Nothing worse than not being in the loop. You never know what you're going to miss. Anyway, I'm sorry, but we don't have a choice at this point. Our plane's taking off in mere minutes and I've got nowhere else to kennel her."

Mention of a kennel brought dogs to Iberia's mind and her gaze turned to me, sitting upright and alert in the Vespa's custom passenger basket.

"Rudolph's gotten fat. Don't feed Haddy the same. Fish fingers twice a day. Peas for greens. Pizza on Fridays. One slice. One topping: pepperoni. And no soda."

She turned to Tony, who looked as if his mind was already poolside sipping a mojito on Paradise Island. He said something in his profoundly Scottish tongue that I believe was both a greeting for my owner and a joke of some kind, but I could not decipher it. I am a multispecies linguist, but Scots is well beyond my power. Iberia had already shifted her attention to Haddy McClay.

"Am I forgetting anything, baby?"

"Yes," Haddy said. "You're forgetting me. I don't want to stay here. What am I going to do for two weeks, play with the stupid dog?"

Tony said something that instantly calmed his offspring down.

"Really?" Haddy said. "Does he really mean it, Mom?"

"Whatever your father says," Iberia said. "God knows no price is too dear." She spoke this last part under her breath and well below the auditory abilities of the surrounding humans.

"But, Ibi," Harry objected. "I really don't know if I can do this."

"C'mon, Harry. It's not as if I ask you every day. In fact, I've never asked you. And besides, your calendar isn't busting at the seams with commitments these days, am I right? Bonding with your niece will do you some good. And it'll be good for Haddy. This has win–win written all over it. We're optimizing here."

Harry was obviously doubtful that anything was "optimizing," but resistance was futile. He had been defeated the moment he saw Iberia parked on 90th Street.

Haddy hugged her parents and stepped out onto the street. Her mother handed her an enormous bag, a teddy bear wearing sunglasses and an instrument case.

Tony revved the engine. Iberia closed the door. Their car began to roll away.

"Oh, and, Harry, don't forget to make Haddy practice."

"Practice what?" Harry asked the fast-disappearing Iberia.

"Her violin, of course," his sister shouted over her shoulder. "It's her ticket to the Ivies."

Harry looked Haddy up and down and sighed.

"My place isn't big like what you're used to in Connecticut," he said.

"I know. Remember, I've seen it. And Mom always calls it Harry's hovel to her friends."

"I guess you'll have to sleep in the bed."

"That's okay. I brought my own sheets."

"How did you know what size bed I've got?"

"I don't," Haddy said. "I've got a selection."

I jumped out of the Vespa and Harry rolled it up onto the sidewalk. He dropped the kickstand and removed the license plate from its Velcro housing.

"That's illegal, isn't it?" Haddy said.

"I have no idea," Harry said.

"You don't know a lot of stuff," Haddy said. "At least, Mom said you don't know a lot of stuff. I've got to make up my own mind about whether you know a lot of stuff or not. I've got to see for myself. I like to see everything for myself. I like to observe. Science is about observing. I like science. Do you have cable?"

Harry nodded.

"Good, I like TV."

Harry's sense of desperation seemed to ease a bit at these words.

"Can you watch a lot of TV?" Harry asked. "Like from morning until you go to bed at night?"

We had just reached our apartment and Harry was turning the key in the door.

"Mom never lets me watch that much TV. She says people who watch a lot of TV don't go to the Ivies. They go to second-tier schools and live second-tier lives, like you."

"Right," Harry said. "But you'd *like* to watch a lot of TV if you could?"

"You betcha," Haddy said, and, moving just short of the speed of light, she had clicked on the television, selected one of those twenty-four-hour child-friendly networks and was rocking back and forth on the La-Z-Boy.

This invasion of our domestic sanctuary was too much. My head spun, my paws felt even weaker than before. The situation seemed well beyond my Labrador's powers to correct. When would I have a moment alone to use the laptop to communicate with my owner and get him back on course if Haddy was to be planted in our midst?

I was about to make my way to my corner when Haddy took notice of me. I tried to scoot past her while shrinking my body as best I could into a smaller target. Alas, I failed, and soon both my ears were in her clammy little-girl hands. She tugged hard again, on the theory that, like my tail, they might also be detachable.

"Doggy," Haddy cooed. "Remember me?"

MY EARS—THOSE DELI-cate, velvety minidrapes that cover the sensitive auditory equipment—were in desperate shape. I could not move for fear that movement would only bring more pain. I could not snap and snarl because it has never been my way to give in to my lower beast-like nature and certainly not on the first day of our guest's fourteen-day stay. Haddy hid my eyes with my ears. Children think this is particularly amusing because they can't do the same with their stiff cartilage. Then, just as Haddy was about to attach a metal binder clip to Yours Truly's left lobe, Harry—who had retreated to the bedroom and was oblivious to the torture of his animal—returned to interrupt her.

"Are you hungry?" Harry asked.

"Starved," Haddy said.

Harry peeked into our deeply troubled refrigerator and emerged with a foodstuff wrapped in clear plastic.

"How about a Ho Ho?" he asked.

The dog's ears were dropped, the Ho Hos received, ripped open and devoured.

"More," Haddy demanded.

"Sorry," Harry said. "That was the last one. I missed it cleaning. I'm allergic to wheat."

"I'm allergic to stuff too. Mom told them that I'm allergic to glue so I don't have to do crafts at school. Mom says people who do crafts don't get into the Ivies. They become craft people, and craft people don't make any money. Got anything else that's like Ho Hos? I really love Ho Hos."

Haddy stretched out in the La-Z-Boy.

"Chocolate anything would be good."

I glanced at Harry and he at me. For a moment there was profound—if silent—interspecies dialogue between us.

"Randolph needs to go for a walk," Harry said. "You'll be okay here, Had, won't you?"

"Can't I come?" Haddy objected. "It's so boring being alone."

I gave my owner a long, pleading stare and hoped it wouldn't be misinterpreted.

"Maybe another time," Harry said. "Randolph

is very shy. He doesn't even like going to the bathroom in front of other dogs."

"That's weird," Haddy editorialized. "Maybe he should see a dog shrink or something."

"Why?"

"For his problem," Haddy said. "Mom says if you have a problem, you fix it. People who don't fix their problems don't—"

"We know," Harry said, interrupting her. "But it's not a problem. It's just part of who Randolph is."

"I guess, but I bet there's a pill for it," Haddy said. "My daddy's on antidepressants."

"I bet," Harry muttered, and opened the door. I made haste to the landing with a kind of saunter (I try never to run), and for a moment it seemed that the problematic child would be left behind. But then the phone rang. It was Detective Davis. He wanted Harry to meet him at the scene of the murder again.

"I'm not staying here," Haddy announced. "There is no way."

I felt certain that Harry would recruit me as babysitter, but instead he looked at both of us and delivered this extraordinary line:

"We'll all ride down on the Vespa."

"Him too?"

"Him too."

"I'll need a helmet," Haddy said. "Motorcycles are dangerous. Mom would kill me if I got brain-damaged."

"This isn't a motorcycle," Harry said. "It's a Vespa. It's a motorcycle dressed in a tuxedo and wearing comfortable slippers. Your brain will be fine. Anyway, you can wear my helmet."

"What will you wear?"

Harry emerged from the bedroom with his water-polo headgear from his college days. He had been a top varsity player.

"Don't be ridiculous, Uncle Harry," Haddy said.

Soon we were all aboard the Vespa and speeding (or, rather, proceeding at a moderate, child-safe clip) downtown.

"I'd exclaim 'whee' if I was the kind of person who exclaimed things like that, but I'm not," said Haddy, who was wedged between my owner and Yours Truly's custom compartment.

Traffic was with us, and even when it was not, our Vespa allowed us to cut through congestion like the proverbial hot knife through butter. Ah, butter. It is a favorite of this Lab's palate.

The yellow tape and police guard were gone when we pulled up in front of the boarding-house. Harry parked the Vespa at the base of the front steps and removed the license plate.

"Lucky I'm not a traffic cop," Detective Davis said, stepping out from behind the stairs. "I'd say you just committed a half dozen moving violations."

"Sorry, Detective, but you made it sound urgent and I wanted to get down here as fast as I could," Harry said.

"I want some Ho Hos," Haddy said.

"Who's the little girl?" Detective Davis asked.

"My niece. It's a long story."

"Let's go inside," the detective said. "It'll only take a minute. You can leave Randolph in the lobby. We're going back to the room."

"If it's okay with you, I'd prefer to take him with me," Harry said.

On the trip downtown, I had wondered why I wasn't left at the apartment. Now I suspected the answer. Harry wanted me to see what he saw. After all, it had only been a few weeks since he was instructed by the "other world" that I had been inspired. Perhaps he was regretting not bringing me on the first expedition.

The first thing I noticed about the lobby was its dizzying overload of scents. My olfactories reeled. I smelled the decades of decline, neglect, vagrancy, dissoluteness and crime. It was as if all the circles of Dante's *Inferno* had telescoped into a single foul-smelling place—a potpourri of

despair. There was also—I began to recognize—
another potent potpourri, of cinnamon, nutmeg
and apple, emanating from dishes discreetly
placed on either side of an old wooden clock
on the mantelpiece. This potpourri was called
"Country Kitchens" and stunned the noses of
man and canine in bed-and-breakfasts across
the country. This veneer of coziness, however,
could not transform the essential nature of the
place. Despite its upscale transformation and
the utopian ideals of its proprietress, the boardinghouse was still a place of transience and
disconnection—an urban way station filled with
alien bodies in separate rooms. The coffee per-
colating on the sideboard, the scones cooling in
a woven basket and the Currier & Ives originals
could not change this fundamental reality. As
if to emphasize the point, two men passed
through the lobby, arguing about a missing
shower cap, and casually stepped over a ragged-
looking man sprawled on the braided rug.

"Goddamn it, Abe, that's what your room's
for," one of the men said.

"It's the poetry," the other man said.

"It's the booze," the first man countered.
"He's been drunk since the Beats."

Abe did not budge, and the two men disappeared down the stairs to the street.

"Is he okay?" Harry asked, stepping around the man.

"He's fine," Detective Davis said. "As I said, you can't take the Bowery out of the boarding-house."

A woman with a clear plastic bag filled with recyclable bottles and cans sat in a wingback easy chair and read *Vogue*.

"Let's go upstairs," Detective Davis said. "There's something else that I want you to see."

"Is it alright for Haddy?" my owner asked.

"Sure. Everything's been cleaned up."

There was one other scent that I could detect beneath the host of conflicting smells. It was Imogen, and as we climbed the stairs toward the room she had occupied for so many months, her scent grew stronger and stronger until, by the time we reached her floor, it was so distinct that I was able to detect scents within that one scent. Just like that moment on the subway stairs a few weeks earlier, there were the major characteristics—the mix of sandalwood, pear and cotton—the "essential" Imogen. And there were also the impermanent qualities—the state-of-mind or mood markers—that I had detected then: fear, deceit and a mother lode of sadness. But there was something else, two recent smells: terror and shock.

How could they be so strong and distinctly hers? I snuffled up deep swaths of carpet following this particular trail—entirely lost in the exercise—until my snout rammed the base of the banister and I was aware of something small and metallic sticking to my nose.

"Randolph, you big goober," Harry said. "What are you doing?"

Detective Davis was more circumspect and more observant.

"There's something stuck to his nose," the detective said. He reached down, removed the object and held it up to the light.

"It's an earring," he said. Detective Davis showed it to Harry.

"It's Imogen's," Harry said. "I bought it for her."

My owner stared at the object. It was a miniature Betty Boop, the bumptious cartoon icon from the 1930s.

"She loved kitsch," Harry said in hushed tones. "I found these at a vintage-clothing store for our first anniversary."

Even Haddy was momentarily respectful.

"Is that that girl you used to like, Uncle Harry?" Haddy asked. "Is that who you're talking about?"

"Yes, Haddy. That's the girl," Harry said.

"Mom didn't like her," Haddy continued. "She said she was stuck up and that she was a thinker, not an achiever."

"Thanks for that, Haddy," Harry said, and turned to Detective Davis. "I guess you folks missed this one—do you want it? I guess it could have dropped here anytime."

"Perhaps, but we found the other one in the victim's hand," Detective Davis said, and began walking toward the room. "I want your opinion on something."

Yellow police tape was strung across the entrance to the room. Detective Davis unlocked the door and ducked under the tape.

"Is it alright for Haddy to come in?" Harry asked. Though I could sense Harry's nerves bristling at seeing Imogen's room again, he did not forget his avuncular responsibility to his difficult niece.

"Sure," Detective Davis confirmed. "Forensics is done. It's like the room's never been lived in, except for this."

Detective Davis switched the ceiling light on, walked over to the window and lowered the blind. Then he herded everyone into the far corner of the room, shut the door and turned the ceiling light off.

"Wow," Harry said.

"Cool," Haddy echoed.

Hundreds of stars appeared on the ceiling—luminous green dots floating in the black.

"It looks like the night sky," Harry said. "It's very complex. Someone spent a lot of time doing this."

"I've got stars on my ceiling at home," Haddy offered. "Except it's the solar system, and now that Pluto's not a planet anymore, it kind of stinks because I like Pluto because it's purple, but it doesn't belong but still I don't want to get rid of it because, like I said, it's purple. I wish it was Mercury that wasn't a planet, not Pluto. But it's not."

"We think Imogen did this, Harry," Detective Davis said when Haddy finally came up for air.

"Why?"

"A few people on the floor remember," Detective Davis said. "Once or twice they walked past and she was standing on the desk sticking these things to the ceiling."

"Why would she have had her door open?" Harry asked.

"That's the way this place is," Detective Davis said. "It's like a dormitory."

"But I thought you said that Imogen and…"

Harry paused. It was difficult to connect our mistress to someone else.

"Yes?"

"I thought you said they didn't mix with the other people here. I mean, wouldn't it be unusual for her to keep the door open?"

"Maybe she wanted some air," Detective Davis said.

"I guess," Harry said. "It just sounds strange."

"You think she wanted people to see her?"

"It's just I know Imogen. I mean, I knew her, and the person I knew liked privacy. She wasn't somebody who kept her door open, especially in a place like this and especially if she was doing something that might draw attention to herself. She hated attention."

"Sounds like a different person," Detective Davis observed. "Don't get me wrong, she was aloof, but people here thought she was a party girl. A lot of comings and goings. All hours. Men asking for her. Waiting around out front. We'd like to talk to some of them, but they seem to have evaporated with the murder. There are two reasons I brought you here again. The first is that the picture that's emerging of Imogen is just not the one I've had, and I think you should be prepared to learn some hard truths about her ahead, Harry. But the second, and the cop-in-me reason, is these stars. I agree with you: I think Imogen wanted people to remember her doing this. Five people on five different occasions saw her doing this. Three of them asked her about it, and she closed the door in their faces without saying a word. And I can tell you from twenty years of police work that if you want somebody to remember something, make them angry or hurt. They'll remember it *and* they'll tell other people about it. For some reason she wanted witnesses to remember her standing on the desk sticking stars to the ceiling."

"But what is it?" Harry asked. "I mean, it's incredibly intricate, but it's as random as the night sky."

"Did she like astronomy?" Detective Davis asked.

"She told me that she had a telescope when she was a kid and used to look at the stars in her backyard in Ohio, but I guess that's not true."

"The geography might not be true," Detective Davis said, "but the details could be substantially the same. This is usually the case with people who want to conceal their origins. Someone said it's hard to be a good liar because you have to remember your lies—it's easier to remember the truth or some close version of it."

Had I the vocal power, I would have supplied Mark Twain as the "someone" Detective Davis meant.

"So it wasn't all made up," Harry said. There was pain close to the surface.

"No, it wasn't all made up," Detective Davis said.

"So what about these stars?"

"I think there's some message in this. It might not be for the NYPD or you, but there's something here."

I scrutinized the ceiling. The points of light wavered against the black background, appearing and disappearing, whole blocks of fluorescent dots turning as if caught in a gentle celestial vortex. It was difficult to focus or find anything like a pattern in this spill of stars. A row of half a dozen on the edge intersected another row of three. They seemed brighter than the rest. Could it be an *L*? Had Imogen built a message into the ceiling? Next to the *L* I thought I could just make out an *O*. But the more I stared, the more letters I saw and the less sense they made. There were no intelligible words beyond nonsense pairs. Perhaps, I thought, switching gears, the stars themselves added up to something, or the stars and the spaces between them served as some kind of Morse code. The dots could be the stars and the dashes the spaces. My musings were interrupted by little Haddy.

"This is so boring," Haddy said. "Mom said you'd be fun, Uncle Harry, but I knew she was lying. 'Cause before that she said you'd been a basket case since that girl left."

Detective Davis switched the lights back on.

"As I said, I think there's a message here, but it would take an army of cryptanalysts to figure this one out, and we don't have that. And we don't have much time either. Someone's moving in here today or tomorrow."

"That's fast," Harry said.

"Ms. Ramsey wanted it. She's the one who runs this place—the one I told you about. She's a saint but she's a character, and she has very strong opinions. Hopefully, we'll make our get-away without an encounter."

"You can't stop her?"

"Yes, but we won't. As I said, we've got all the forensics."

"But what about the stars?"

"We've got photographs. It's not the same

thing, but it should be enough. Anyway, we've requested that they not be removed from the ceiling for a month or so. But who knows? This is New York. Nothing stays the same for very long."

THE STARS PROVIDED A concrete link to my mistress and more proof that she was trying to communicate something essential. But to whom? Perhaps it was only to posterity or for her own sanity and sense of self. Preserving the photograph on the dresser but eliminating Harry so the context would not be identifiable might also be explained this way. But if it was just an act of memory or defiance, why allow witnesses?

My thoughts returned to Imogen's journal and its code. The code had been a simple cipher and spelled *Cymbeline*. Harry had ultimately cracked it after my analysis led nowhere, but only I had understood the connection to the action of the Shakespearean play *Cymbeline* and Imogen's namesake, a central character who feigns her own death to protect those she loves from malevolent forces. For a brief moment, I

had the shocking idea that Imogen had in-
tended me to be the audience and the code
solver. To grasp this significance and somehow
pass it on. But this made no sense. After all, I
might be a loyal dog in her mind, but I was certainly still just a dog.

We left Detective Davis at the boardinghouse and climbed aboard the Vespa for the trip
home. I burrowed deep in my compartment so
that I could sift through the scents I had gathered from the room. There wasn't much that
was useful. Imogen's scent was strong, but it did
not add much to what I already knew. I was certain of one thing, but this was no surprise: my
mistress had not been romantically involved
with the dead man. Nor had she slept in the
room very often—at least not in recent months.

It was now even more urgent that I communicate what I knew to Harry, but the prospect
of doing this in the near future looked unlikely
because of the presence of Haddy McClay. But
then I was granted a chance.

"I'm hungry," Haddy said as we turned onto
the 90th Street home stretch. "I want fish
sticks."

"I don't have any," Harry said.

"Well, we've got to get some. Fish sticks are
basically all I eat. I adore fish sticks," Haddy

said. I suspected that someone had been reading a bit too much *Eloise* to our precocious
youngster. Harry, however, didn't seem to notice
the literary allusion and instead focused on how
to answer the demand without polluting our
newly wheat-free abode.

"I'm taking you out," he finally said. "We'll go
to the Gotham Diner on Broadway. You'll love
it. A real New York experience."

"They better have fish sticks," Haddy muttered.

"First, Randolph goes upstairs," Harry said.

"I'll stay right here," Haddy announced.

"No you won't," Harry said. "The last thing I
need to tell your mom is that I lost you."

"She wouldn't mind," Haddy said.

"Of course she would," Harry said.

"No, really, she wouldn't," Haddy maintained.
"She's always saying some women aren't cut out
to be mothers and that she's one of them."

Ten minutes later, Yours Truly was seated at
the kitchen table in the serene emptiness of
our apartment. Harry's computer had been
powered up with a snout-wipe. I had observed
Harry navigating the virtual environment, but
now that it was my turn, I knew this would be a

challenge. There is a part of any advanced animal that imagines itself free from the prison of the body. Humans, unlike dogs, have ample dexterity. I had imagined using my paws like some cartoon dog—tapping away at the keyboard with my tongue a-wag. This was not to be. Like cereal work, the computer would be a snout job—painstaking and precise. Fortunately, the keys were relatively large and the DELETE button prominent.

The keyboard would matter most when I had messages to write, and I wanted those messages to come from an outside source. I would play on my owner's supernatural soft spot once again—much as I disliked encouraging this bad behavior—and send him e-mails from a spirit guide. I had toyed with the idea of composing the messages directly on his computer, but I balked. Only recently had I watched a *National Geographic* team on television sedate a harbor seal for "its own good" and attach a camera to its head. I didn't fancy becoming Exhibit B in the dog-brain department at MIT, so it seemed wise to cover my tracks in some way.

My damp nose skidded across the touch pad (I tried not to think of the human germs festering there), and with laborious but steady progress, I moved the digital arrow around the desktop, imitating the actions Harry had taken to get online. I was successful and soon had a window open. This took me through the registration process for my e-mail account. I entered the following:

> First Name: Randolph
> Last Name: Labrador
> Gender: Male
> Birth Date: 11/14/1970

The reader will note that I took some creative license with my birth date. I originally entered my calendar birth year but was informed that I would need my parents' permission to complete the registration. In any case, I told the approximate truth in dog years.

A few clicks more and it was done. *Astudyinscarlet1887@hotmail.com* was ready to communicate. The name was a reference to Conan Doyle's first Sherlock Holmes mystery, published in *Beeton's Christmas Annual* in 1887, and underscored the identity of a wise detective spirit guide—the same mastermind who had employed Alpha-Bits so effectively. My own identity would remain cloaked and known only to the operators of the Web site, and what they would know would be quite vague.

I heard footsteps on the stairs. Communication would have to wait. At first the footsteps sounded like Harry's, but then I realized that they were heavier and there was no little girl in tow. Perhaps it was some other occupant of our walk-up apartment, but they stopped at our door. The door handle jiggled. The door was pushed in and then pulled out. I closed the window and nosed the laptop's lid shut just as something metallic was thrust into the lock. The tool moved about inside the lock and manipulated the tumblers. *Click...click...click...*

I began to sweat between my toes. Our lock was supposed to be secure against such assaults, but one by one I heard the tumblers fail. I approached the door and produced a low growl, but the person on the other side did not pause or even slow the work. Another tumbler failed. I considered retreating to the bedroom, but before I could move, the lock turned and the front door swung open.

"G'DAY, POOCH," AN ENOR-
mous man wearing an Akubra hat
said as he stepped into our apartment and shut the door behind him. "You must
be Randolph. I've heard a lot about you from
your mistress."

He reached down and gave my head a most
agreeable tousle with his giant hand. The man
spoke with a distinct Australian accent and I
knew that this was the menacing figure from
Christmas night the previous year. The scent
matched. That night Harry and I had been returning from dinner at Jackson's and had—so it
seemed at the time—only narrowly avoided a
confrontation with this figure, who stalked us
from the shadows on the desolate street and
away from whom I finally managed to pull my
owner. Now I also suspected that this man was
the guardian of the fortune Iris had spoken
about before she died. This guardian, she had

told us, was an Australian lawyer entrusted with determining the worthiness of the fortune's inheritor and he would be coming to meet us soon. Nothing in his scent was threatening, and I wondered whether I had overreacted when my owner and I encountered him on Central Park West that dark night.

The man surveyed the apartment and his eyes settled on the La-Z-Boy.

"Think I'll wait for your young man in the rocker," he announced. "It looks like a ripper."

He lowered his monumental frame into the chair and let out a similarly monumental sigh—the kind of legendary exhalation that I imagined mythic figures might make. A Norse god sort of sigh.

A word seems necessary on dog territoriality. The reader might think it odd that I did not fly into a frenzy over this intrusion into our abode. But territoriality is a lot like nationalism in human beings: it occurs in varying degrees. Yours Truly, who naturally leans to the philosophical, considers the impermanence of our existence as the basic benchmark for his responses. As Detective Davis so aptly observed: in New York nothing stays the same for very long. Any apartment, including ours, is more temporary encampment than citadel. That said, when the man tried to put the footrest up, I growled a second time.

He laughed but desisted.

"Your master's sanctuary, huh, mate? I understand," he said, correctly grasping the purpose of my growl. "You don't mind if I watch telly, though?"

He smiled and turned on the television. A ghost-hunting program was on, and to my surprise—we had heard nothing of this project— Harry's friend Ivan Manners was leading a camera crew into a "haunted" mustard factory in Queens. Mr. Apples was perched on his shoulder and Ivan's mouth ran without stopping.

"Now, rumor has it that if you stand beneath Vat Number Three, where Orange B is added to the mustard mixture, you will hear—if you're really lucky—the spectral cries of one ill-fated Tobias H. Smith, who managed Vat Number Three until the day he plummeted to his death by drowning in its sticky contents . . ."

"What rubbish," the man said, and flipped through the channels until he found a twenty-four-hour news station. The anchor moved from a story on civil strife in the Congo to the exploits of a drunken former child star.

"There is no truth anymore, Randolph. Only hype and the power of your spin. And these daffy bastards call themselves journalists. Most of them aren't worth warm spit," he said.

I heard Harry and Haddy McClay on the stairs. Haddy was complaining about the fish sticks at the diner. I considered positioning myself at the front door and barking. The behavior would certainly alert Harry, but to what advantage? The enormous man in the La-Z-Boy gave me no indication that he posed a threat. Then another thought came to mind. What if Harry was carrying Grandfather Oswald's WWII–era .45? An image of my owner bursting through the doorway on the strength of his usually reticent Labrador's warning barks and shooting the Australian dead in the La-Z-Boy was sobering. It was also unwarranted, since a moment later I remembered that the NYPD had confiscated the weapon after Iris's death.

Harry fumbled with the keys. The Australian glanced at the door but did not budge from the La-Z-Boy. He seemed very relaxed.

The door swung open. Harry saw the man and froze.

"Harry, it's good to finally meet you," the man said, delivering a smile and a wave and turning the entire spirit of their meeting from criminal to pleasantly social merely by the strength of his personality.

"Who the hell are you?" Harry asked, instinctively pushing Haddy back into the hall. Then he looked down at me with a somewhat disparaging expression that suggested he was not happy to see me sitting next to this stranger in the La-Z-Boy.

"Randolph, come here, for God's sake."

"He's a special pup, that one," the man noted as he rose to his feet with some effort against the powerful gravity of the addictive La-Z-Boy.

"That chair's a ripper. I reckon you don't need a bed."

As tall as my owner is, the Australian had a few inches on him. He advanced with his arm outstretched for a handshake.

"My name's Malcolm Patterson, and I'm your new best friend," the man said. "Me friends call me Blinko."

"Why?"

"Because when I was a kid, I got hot ashes in my eye, and after I got my sight back I couldn't stop blinking. Aussies love their nicknames. Ha."

"Why are you in my apartment?" Harry asked. "How did you get into my apartment?"

"I picked the lock," Blinko explained.

"That's breaking and entering."

"Just entering...I didn't break a thing,"

Blinko said. "I'm always doing it back home with locking myself out and the like."

"We don't do that in America," Harry said. "At least not if we want to stay out of jail."

"Do you have any Ho Hos?" Haddy interjected, poking her head between Harry's arm and the door frame.

"Come inside," Blinko said. "It's no good standing out in the hall."

"This is crazy," Harry said, but came inside anyway.

"You should close the door," Blinko said.

"Not until I know what this is about."

"I told you," Blinko said. "I'm your new best friend. We need to team up. There are some dodgy forces at work."

"I don't even know what this is about," Harry said. But then he understood. "You're the keeper of the fortune. You're the one that Iris talked about."

"'The keeper of the fortune' sounds like bollocks. There isn't a myth here—only money. Money and power. The Great Game—the game that governments and corporations play with one another and sacrifice the little people doing it."

"So there is a fortune," Harry said. "Iris wasn't crazy."

"No, she was a genuine nutter, Harry. She just

got a few of the facts right. The word *fortune* makes it sound like a good thing when it's really a burden, an obligation, something that puts you on the spot when you'd rather be left alone. It's put your Imogen on the spot."

"What do you know?" Harry asked.

"Shut the door and I'll tell you, mate," Blinko said.

"I have a better idea," Harry said. "Let's go for a walk. Randolph needs to do his Numbers."

"I'd prefer to stay indoors," Blinko said. "Have you ever heard of a Heckler and Koch PSG-1?"

"It sounds like a gun," Harry said.

"It is a gun. One of the most accurate sniper rifles in the world. A shooter positioned on a building across the park could split an apple on the sidewalk in front of your building. Word has it that there are a number of PSG-1s floating about New York these days attached to characters with permission to use them. It's a good idea to avoid the open during the day."

"Are you suggesting that there is someone out there on top of a building somewhere ready to pop you off?" Harry asked. "New York isn't a war zone."

"Harry, there is always a war going on around

you; you've just grown up unaware of it," Blinko said.

Haddy pushed past both of them and turned on the television.

"This is boring," she said. "I want to watch TV."

"Only a miserable child would think that the prospect of having one's noggin turned to mush by a sniper's bullet was boring. I've seen blue-tongued skinks with more native curiosity."

Harry looked at Blinko.

"I don't know whether to call the police or buy you a drink," Harry said.

"Call the police if you like, but our problems are much bigger than the locals. They can't help us much now," Blinko said. "I'll go for the walk."

"But I thought you said it wasn't safe," Harry said.

"I just wanted to open your mind up to the hazards of your new life," Blinko said. "Besides, it's getting dark now."

HARRY ATTACHED MY leash and our strange, somewhat jumpy party headed to the bridle path that runs around the reservoir. Haddy McClay had been much chastened by Blinko's words and slunk behind the adults as we made our way toward Central Park. Harry was distracted and took three doggy disposal bags from the courtesy dispenser at the end of our block. New York suddenly seemed much less secure. People passing us on the street took on a suspicious cast. Two Yorkshire terriers bore down on me with almost militant fervor before their owner dragged them off in the opposite direction.

"Leave it," their owner commanded, using the rather offensive dog-training terminology that has now become ubiquitous on our island. I am not an "it," and few dogs are stupid enough to mistake me for a dropped hamburger or a dead bird. Yes, Yours Truly's nerves were on full alert. Blinko's theoretical sniper's bullet hung somewhere in the Manhattan air, stayed only mometarily from speeding toward its target.

We crossed Central Park West, dipped down the small path beside the 90th Street gate and then up and over the hillock and across the road until we were walking under the trees on a grass-covered trail to the bridle path. It was early evening and several dogs were out with their owners for the "after-work" walk, snuffling the rich soils beneath the trees and among the shrubbery and racing in lines and circles through the leaves and wood chips. Blinko was the kind of man who saw without seeming to look, and I could sense that whatever reluctance he had to coming outside had diminished in this crowd and he was now well at ease.

Harry let me off my leash.

"Go on, Randolph, do your business," Harry said. At his words, I noticed a certain bladder-based urgency that I had ignored, but I hesitated since I did not want to miss any of what Blinko might have to say to my owner while attending to my so-called business. Making matters more complicated, our party had stopped in the middle of the path, and as usual my *Foliage-Finder* nature prevented me from the public leg lift.

Needless to say, the *Squat-and-Drops* were out in full force and delivering seemingly endless quantities of "presents" for their owners to scurry at with doggy disposal bags worn like catcher's mitts. Of course, while the *Earth-Onlys*—the hippies of the canine world—were enjoying themselves in this narrow wilderness between road and reservoir, the *Asphalt-Onlys* were craving the nearest stretch of blacktop.

All dogs are compulsives to a greater or lesser extent. We have these requirements for our Numbers. And we have our odd dances, shakes and movements that are often habitual. One dog scuffs up the dirt with its hind legs after a Number 2; another rubs its right shoulder against the base of a tree or executes a half roll. Compulsivity might be classified as a neurosis in the human world, but in the dog world it is a form of sanity—after all, it is an attempt to repeat something in a universe that embraces the random and complete something in defiance of the perpetual loose end. When these habits are interrupted or threatened, a dog can lose its sense of proportion. Just as I was about to head off to the shrubbery—it seemed likely that I'd be back before Blinko had shared anything of import with my owner—an *Asphalt-Only*, shaky from blacktop deprivation, approached for the customary hindquarter sniff and information exchange. This sniff practice is revolting, a primitive holdover from pack days. It is also unnecessary, since the same information can be gleaned by a more thoughtful olfactory survey of the air, which doesn't require one dog's nose shoved into the other's rump. I pivoted away, deflecting the *Asphalt-Only*'s approaching snout. Unfortunately, the *Asphalt-Only* was a Maltese terrier–Chihuahua mix with a fierce Latin nature (the kind of temperament Thomas Mann spent pages puzzling over in his fictional works). The dog did not appreciate my maneuver and delivered a quick snarl and a yap-screech that stunned the ear. From a distance his owner cried out.

"Leave it, General Franco. Leave it."

But General Franco did not "leave it." Instead, he jumped into the air and clamped his little incisors into the side of my mouth. The pain was sharp and my reaction lamentable. My lower nature assumed command, and in an instant I was holding General Franco in my jaws like an oversized chew toy.

"Randolph, drop him," Harry said.

General Franco squirmed. Though trapped and his neck contorted, he did not surrender or release the side of my mouth. We were locked in a stalemate. His owner arrived seconds later, a generously proportioned woman wearing a T-shirt that proclaimed her status as *Disco Queen of New York*. Harry, Blinko and the Disco Queen stood mute before the image of her animal in my jaws. Haddy McClay alone made a comment.

"Cool," she said.

I frequently find that my philosophic disposition rescues me from the brutal reality playing out around me. Such was the case now as General Franco's incisors became the focus of a brief meditation on the subject of pain. At the core of the question of pain (and, indeed, its opposite, pleasure) is the idea of permanence. Pain fluctuates. It is not a constant. General Franco's incisors in the delicate skin of my mouth were initially a terrible thing. Now they were mere nuisance. But emotional pain—or, better, pain of the mind—has a different nature: it does not have such clear dimensions, such easily seen ebbs and flows. Imogen's disappearance was a chronic condition, and this dog knew neither Harry nor I would rest until we had one single good answer to all that had happened: a unified theory of loss. And, more important, until our mistress was back.

I dropped General Franco and focused my

mind on the excruciating, but limited, reality of his incisors digging a deep, raw trench into my mouth as he swung trapezelike onto the ground.

"Good boy," Harry said. He apologized to the Disco Queen, who insisted that General Franco was to blame.

"Wasn't he always," Blinko muttered under his breath, making pointed reference to the problematic historical figure without whom the world would never have been treated to Picasso's *Guernica*.

When the Disco Queen and her charge had vanished, Blinko bent down and gave my wound a quick look.

"She'll be apples, mate," he said, clapping me on the back while he dispensed the vigorous Australian idiom, which, roughly translated, means *As severe as things might appear, there is nothing to worry about, and if deadly infection sets in we'll take another look but won't be in any hurry about it.* Yes, they are a rugged people.

Sensing that any serious discussion was momentarily derailed, I hastened to the foliage on the opposite side of the path and found privacy behind a London plane tree. Afterward, I lingered for a moment to inhale the rich bouquet of an early-spring mushroom mingling with a clutch of crocus. I floated among these exquisite smells and gave a head-to-tail shake and stretch. I, like George Santayana, the notable Harvard professor and poet, had been late for my "appointment with spring." Thus, restored and with the pain of my wound diminishing—the clean environment of a dog's mouth is indeed curative—I returned to Harry and Blinko, who were beginning to discuss serious things.

"You did the right thing shooting Iris, you know," Blinko said, offering an assessment that the enormous man from the outback must have considered something of an icebreaker.

"I don't know," Harry said.

"She was a monster," Blinko said. "I knew her from the beginning. Not everyone you'll be meeting will be so cut and dry."

"She was cut and dry?" Harry asked.

"Once you knew the beast, yes, she was cut and dry: an evil nutter," Blinko said.

I noted how Blinko spoke with an almost prophetic hush at times, as if my owner was already on a mission whether he liked it or not. It was as if Blinko knew the course of the weeks and months ahead and was only the first of the many characters we were to meet in this strange new world that was opening up to us. My owner noticed this dimension as well and to my surprise addressed it directly.

"I don't know why you seem to think I am part of this," Harry said. "I'm not your new best friend. I'm at the end of this chapter of my life. Not at the beginning. Imogen has moved on and so have I. She's not the person I thought she was. She's involved in bad things. Maybe she's even done bad things."

Blinko was silent. Haddy McClay had run a few yards off and been momentarily adopted by a family playing a twilight game of catch. Finally, the enormous man spoke. It was like the door of a vault had been opened, carrying a rich cargo of knowledge up and out on a rush of air.

"She told me you'd be true blue," Blinko said. "And instead all I find is light blue, china blue, powder blue."

"She's the one who's not committed," Harry said. "She's the one who's been shacking up with someone else."

Blinko didn't answer this charge, although it was terribly clear that Harry wanted and needed it answered.

Instead, he waved his hand as if to dismiss my owner.

"No worries, mate," Blinko said. "I'll be on my way, and if you're lucky you'll get out of this with your life—but I wouldn't wager on it. You've been a bit too close to the flame for too long. And Imogen, of course, she'll be dead. That goes without saying. But you're over her, aren't you? She's not your responsibility anymore."

Harry drew the point of his shoe across the ground between them.

"She's not the woman that I thought she was," Harry said. "And for all I know you could be involved with what happened down at that boardinghouse. My God, you broke into my apartment. How legitimate is that? And if you care about her, what is stopping you from helping?"

Blinko sighed.

"I'm not sure I like you. I don't know if you're the right sort," he said. "But I'm short on options. I will tell you as much of the story as I know and I hope it is enough."

Harry nodded. I sat down on my haunches and listened.

"I'M A LAWYER BY TRAIN-
ing, but I'm a Jackaroo by inclina-
tion and upbringing," Blinko said.
"A Jackaroo is what you Yanks call a cowboy, but
without the guns. My home is the flats, the dry
expanses of Australia where the droughts are
measured in decades. Now, I had a good friend
and he was very wealthy because of his father's
pure luck."

"Iris told the story," Harry said. "Her grandfather was flying a plane and found the largest
reserve of uranium…"

"The largest in the world," Blinko said. "In all
of human history. And the bugger found it without even trying. His son was my friend, whose
daughter was Iris, the aforementioned nutter.
Iris's daughter was Imogen. Now, Imogen was
raised in secret to keep her safe from Iris—
that's why the past you probably thought you
knew was a bit exaggerated."

"More than exaggerated," Harry said. "A lie. Austria isn't Akron."

"Yep, a bit of a fibberoo, but it kept her alive," Blinko said.

"I would never have told anyone," Harry said.

Blinko nodded. "She was used to the other version."

"Why didn't your friend raise her himself like any normal grandfather would do?"

"I asked him that myself," Blinko said. "But Dolpho wasn't that normal either."

"Dolpho?" Harry said. "That's a funny name."

"Australians abbreviate everything and add an *O*," Blinko explained. "His full name was Randolph."

My ears instinctively pricked up at my name.

"Randolph?" Harry asked. "You mean she named Randolph after her grandfather?"

"That's right," Blinko said. "Understandable, since she never met him. If she had, she might have thought different. We always idealize what we don't know well. Randolph was a difficult man to get along with. I did because I had known him for yonks, since we were tots. Long story short: when Iris went bad, Dolpho was wounded, though he never said it. He struck out on the trail and followed his father's uranium lode from the south to the north. Then he walked it east to west. He did it solo. Searching out water. Searching out food. Becoming a creature of the bush. He was out there alone for the better part of a year, and when he came back he looked an utter wreck but that land was his. Australia's an ancient place, and it works on you if you let it. And it had worked on Dolpho. He had heard its voice about permanence and how small a man is. How insignificant. It warped him a bit the other way. He came back convinced it wasn't just dumb luck that his father found that uranium in a bloomin' airplane. It had his sweat all over it now. His hunger. His loneliness. The land had been his constant companion. It was his. That's what he told us. So one day I got a call. I was still a relatively young lawyer then. Dolpho asked whether it was possible to create a trust that would bypass Iris—whose whereabouts were unknown—and go to Imogen, who was a little girl now being raised by nannies in Paris. He didn't want *what had become his* precious uranium to go to anyone really, but he had limited options. And he wanted something extra built into the trust."

"He didn't want Imogen to have it until she was thirty," Harry said.

"Yes, Dolpho wanted to make sure that she wasn't a nutter too, and he wanted this to be a guarantee," Blinko said. "And being this man's friend, I agreed. Two decades later, Dolpho is long dead and I find myself stuck in this city assessing a young woman whose own grandfather never bothered to visit. But Dolpho's reach was long and my hands are tied. He kept me as a watcher. I can assess but I can't get directly involved, and if I do get involved I will be replaced by another trustee. At this point—for reasons I'm not at liberty to say—that would be disastrous."

"So Imogen can't inherit until she is thirty, and if she's crazy, the uranium..."

"Reverts to the government of Australia," Blinko said. "Not just if she's crazy, though. I think she's passed that test. She's not crazy like her mother. No, there is something more pressing right now. If she's arrested on suspicion of murder, that's it. As much as Dolpho loved that uranium, he was deeply ashamed of Iris and would rather have seen the government get it than let it support the life of another psychopath."

"It sounds like a complicated family," Harry said. "I'm surprised Imogen is so normal."

"She was raised far enough away," Blinko said. "All she had was the sense of loss instead of the up-close example of madness. She had love anyway. There were those nannies in France who raised her most of the way—they loved her and she loved them. One in particular. But that's another story. Right now I need you to help her and help us. As far as I can tell, when Imogen disappeared that day, she went underground. This worked for a while, but then things began to catch up with her. There was Iris, for one, thanks to Overton, whose reporting skills helped Iris find her daughter. But that was only part of it. Then the big boys entered. There are a dozen or so nations and/or large multinationals that would like to get their hands on what might be coming to Imogen. For many years, the uranium has gone unmined. The market has been weak, and digging it up and exporting it wasn't economical. There were also some very tough governmental controls. Both of those things have changed: the battle for energy sources and weapons fuel has driven the price through the roof, and the government has changed its tune. Needless to say, Imogen is a much-sought-after young lady. For a number of months Imogen managed to stay missing, but it seems then one or more of the big boys tracked her down and everything changed."

The enormous man drew a deep breath. Nothing in Blinko's scent suggested deceit.

Haddy McClay, playing catch in near dark, dropped the ball and loudly blamed the thrower. Harry traced another line in the dirt with his foot.

"These people will use anything at their disposal to coerce Imogen to turn over her rights to the uranium, and she has played them against one another."

"But what about the dead guy?" Harry asked. "Clearly she's had favorites."

"I don't know much about him," Blinko said. "My guess is that he knew something that the others didn't and she had to keep him especially close, but I don't know."

"But she's not in any danger," Harry said. "After all, if she's gone, then so are their chances of getting what they want."

"Yes, but I believe you might be in danger," Blinko said. "They learned about the details of the trust, and given that there are a limited number of copies of the document in secure locations, this was no mean feat. I am certain that the stakes have been raised in this game. One or more of the parties is no longer content to let Imogen play hard to get. They want to force her hand even if it means losing—but I am sure they are quite convinced they won't lose. Imogen didn't murder that bloke. They did—whoever they are. And now whatever control she had is overturned. She is on the run. The evidence might justify her arrest, and her arrest alone would put her claim to the fortune in jeopardy."

"But why would she care? Imogen was never materialistic," Harry asked.

"She'd still have this killing hanging over her. I'm sure she's going on instinct right now, and it's telling her to keep moving until she can get some clarity," Blinko said. "So she's on the run again and they hold her only way out. They could clear her. But, of course, they won't unless she agrees to their terms. And even then I'm not so sure."

"What do you mean?" Harry asked.

"Remember, this is a competition. There are different sides here. It's possible that some of them want the uranium turned over to the Australian government, because the government won't run it themselves. They'll sell the concession to someone who'll mine it for them—there's still a lot of money to be made that way. Of course, most of them would prefer to own it themselves, but business is business; it's just a question of better returns."

"My God, she's in deep," Harry said.

"She's quite a girl," Blinko said. "She's a little battler. But I've gone as far as I can. I know what the situation is, but if I try to track her down—not that I could, mind you—or I get involved, I'd be compromised. But *you* can do something."

"Get shot by some unseen sniper," Harry said.

"Oh, forget about that; I was just trying to get your attention. No one'll try to kill you—at least not yet," Blinko said.

"So what can I do?"

"You can solve the murder."

"How?" Harry asked.

"That boardinghouse is filled with characters, and some of them are players in this game. But there are four in particular, and one of those four buggers did the killing, I'm certain of it. They are agents for some country or some corporation. They were living there to keep track of Imogen. Everyone was angling to get near her, and they were the closest suitors."

"But she's gone now," Harry said. "Why aren't they?"

"It'd be too suspicious," Blinko said. "And, besides, you'll find that they have day jobs—all of them to the man are affiliated in some way with the United Nations—and the boardinghouse is near the six train, an easy commute to work. Even assassins can save taxi fare. They're all

somewhere in the diplomatic food chain—
mostly the lower rungs."

"And how am I supposed to get near them?"
Harry asked. "You want me to move in?"

"No," Blinko said. "I want your dog to move
in and I want you to visit often."

The Australian handed Harry a business card.

"Leopold Maranovsky," Harry read. "Who is
Leopold Maranovsky?"

"Mr. Maranovsky is the agoraphobic press
secretary for the small but cultured nation of
Near Upper Pilasia."

"I've never heard of it," Harry said.

"You wouldn't have," Blinko said. "It is a small
borderland nation whose chief exports are illu-
minated manuscripts and hot-water bottles. A
place that is swallowed up a dozen times a century by its neighbors, only to reemerge as an au-
tonomous nation again and again. This man is
moving into Imogen's room at the boardinghouse tomorrow. He is in desperate need of a
therapy dog, and Randolph must provide that
service. He is expecting a call from you. It is all
organized."

BLINKO DISAPPEARED into the night, and Harry made the call to Mr. Leopold Maranovsky when we returned to our apartment. He arranged to meet Maranovsky at the boardinghouse early the next morning. Maranovsky explained that he had just arrived in the country but had been prevented from bringing his own dog to carry out the job of calming the diplomatic attaché. Then Harry remembered that in all the excitement we had missed the vet appointment that he had scheduled online.

"Oh well. I'll reschedule soon," Harry said to me. "It can't be too dire."

Haddy McClay went to sleep in the bedroom after Harry changed the sheets and turned on two of Imogen's Twelve Apostle night-lights, thinking that Haddy would welcome their comforting glow.

"I'm not into night-lights," Haddy said. "If it's not pitch black I can't sleep a wink."

"When I was your age," Harry said, "I couldn't stand the dark. I was afraid of it. It always felt like it was closing in. And there were monsters under the bed."

"Really?" Haddy said. "That's kind of pathetic. I'm special. I'm a child insomniac."

As if to emphasize this point, she donned eyeshades.

"Good night, Uncle Harry."

"Good night," Harry said. He closed the door and settled himself into the La-Z-Boy. In a few minutes he was asleep.

Only I stayed awake, puzzling through all that was said and smelled in the exchange between my owner and Blinko. Nothing in Blinko seemed dishonest. He might have been holding back parts of the truth, but, if he was, they weren't parts that mattered directly to us now. The light of the full moon spread slowly across the floor of my little corner. Blinko was what he seemed to be, I concluded, an old man who looked younger than his age, but still an old man who had become entangled in something because of friendship, loyalty and a basically good nature and now wanted to discharge his duties and go home without losing his integrity in the process. Blinko, Harry and I had a mess to clean up. A quotation from one of the greats, Edgar Allan Poe, came to mind: *The true genius shudders at incompleteness—and usually prefers silence to saying something which is not everything it should be.* Poe, when he wasn't worrying about being buried alive or losing money at cards, made sure to be complete in his work. He had poetry. Poetry makes it easy. Art you can finish. Life is different. Life drags on and defies resolution. Even geniuses struggle with life. The only geniuses at living life are those who—half asleep—can shape it into a kind of completeness and forget about all the loose ends. I drowsed in the shadow of these unpromising reflections.

The next morning, Harry, Haddy McClay and I arrived at the boardinghouse at a quarter to nine to meet my temporary charge, Leopold Maranovsky. Harry was going to leave me and continue on with his niece to his first day on the job of the mosaic commission at WAHA. We did not have to search for Maranovsky. A man in a poorly tailored suit sat on the steps of the boardinghouse with a large trunk at his feet. He had a jowly face and large brown eyes. He was a sad-looking man who gave the impression that he was about to sigh. When he saw us, he rose to his feet and suddenly looked happy, but he kept the trunk between himself and us like a shield.

"I was so afraid that you would not come. You are two minutes late. I was on the verge of panic," Maranovsky said.

"Sorry," Harry said.

"I would never manage to travel in one of those vehicles. Never," Maranovsky said. "They are so terribly open. My God, I would die. Just die."

Harry flicked the kick-stand and told Haddy McClay to stay on the bike.

"Here he is, Mr. Maranovsky," Harry said, shaking the press secretary's right hand and placing my leash in his left. "Randolph is particularly good at alleviating anxiety. He is my best dog."

Maranovsky scrutinized me.

"Near Upper Pilasian retrievers have flatter heads. He looks like Near Lower Pilasian or Near Middle Pilasian retriever. Yes, indeed, eyes are quite like Near Lower Pilasian," he decided with a classic Slavic disregard for the definite and indefinite articles of the English language.

"He's a Labrador," Harry clarified.

"Yes, yes, precisely. It is only matter of—what you say—semantics. He is calm dog?"

"A cool cucumber," Harry said.

"Good," Maranovsky said. "Because I am not very cool cucumber."

The press secretary laughed but gave my owner an embattled look.

"Everywhere I see danger," Maranovsky said. "The anxiety began when I was fifty, and, as I believe I said on telephone last night, only the presence of dog removes it from me. I may have him for two weeks, no?"

"Yes," Harry said, although I detected in his voice—or hope I detected—great reluctance to leave me with an utter stranger.

"Perfect," Maranovsky said. He bent down and affixed a purple ribbon to my collar that proclaimed me: *Therapy Dog.* "I shall move in, then. Would you mind carrying the trunk?"

Before Harry had a chance to respond, the press secretary had disappeared up the stairs and through the front door, with me in tow. Harry followed behind with Haddy McClay, whom he could not leave unattended on the city street. Harry pushed the case into the lobby with a grunt and said his good-byes lest he be recruited to carry it the remaining three flights.

"Good-bye, Mr. Maranovsky. Good-bye, Randolph," Harry said. "I'll be checking in regularly, and you have my phone."

I made eye contact with my owner. He

looked pained and uncertain about leaving me. Nevertheless, Harry managed to deliver a professional pat on the head, tell me to "do my job" and disappear through the door.

"It is just us now, my friend," Mr. Maranovsky said, and approached a small closetlike niche in the corner that resembled a coat check but served as a front desk. "Let us see about checking in. Ms. Ramsey is expecting us."

There was a small silver bell on the counter and the press secretary rang it several times in quick succession. As the rings receded, I heard two sounds. The first was the 150cc motor of Harry's Vespa revving to life and the vehicle speeding my owner and Haddy McClay away to points north on its twelve-inch wheels. The second sound was footsteps approaching us from down a long hall. They were light footsteps but distinct and swiftly moving, like a tidy flood. A woman turned the corner and approached, smoothing her apron and slowing almost imperceptibly to examine herself as she passed a mirror on the wall.

"Mr. Maranovsky," the woman said. "I am Ms. Ramsey. We are so pleased to be able to accommodate you. Was your trip pleasant?"

My temporary employer took Ms. Ramsey's extended hand in his own and delivered a kiss with exaggerated elegance, as if he were greeting royalty and not the proprietress of a once-seedy boardinghouse.

"Oh, Mr. Maranovsky. What lovely old-world manners," Ms. Ramsey tittered, as if *she* had just been reading a Jane Austen novel. New York is a city that plays against type. The taxi driver is a Joyce scholar. The academic-looking man will hit you with a tire iron and run off with your wallet. It is also a city of second and third chances, glorious reinvention and magical holes in the wall that one could never predict. Some version of Narnia's wardrobe hides behind every doorway or flight of stairs. I am not sure what I expected in the proprietress of this establishment, but it wasn't Ms. Ramsey. She stepped through a low door and behind the desk.

"I see you have brought your pet," Ms. Ramsey said. "He will be most welcome. In addition to afternoon tea for our human guests, we have an animal smorgasbord on the sunporch. My father was a zoologist, you see, and he fostered in me a deep love and respect for our animal brethren. He was convinced of their intelligence and their infinite goodness. Not all of them, of course—he couldn't brook squirrels, but that was because of a traumatic experience in his childhood."

"I love animals also," the gentle and courtly Leopold responded. "It is my human colleagues whom I find hard to love."

"Oh, Mr. Maranovsky, you must look for the good and you will find it."

Ms. Ramsey smiled and jotted something down.

"This is wonderful place," Leopold said. "It feels like home."

"It is a home," Ms. Ramsey said. "I was raised here and I have never left. My father bought it as an investment when he was at the university. Then there were his controversial experiments. He was a man ahead of his time, Mr. Maranovsky."

"Leopold, please."

"Leopold, my father was a genius, and if a genius does not have the good fortune of escaping the gravity of this world's standards—like Einstein and others escaped to the divine above—then they are slowly crushed by the mundane and the unimaginative. This happened to my father. But he was such an optimist until the end, poor soul. And a lover of animals. Our home—this place—was filled with animals of all sorts, including seven of us children. They all fled—the children—my brothers and sisters, that is. The animals were eventually taken by the city—not all of them, mind you, just the ones that violated the health code. And then Daddy and Mommy died. But I stayed and kept the place running through those terrible years—the 1970s—when New York almost gave up on herself. Now New York is back, and we are here to celebrate it and extend welcome to wonderful people from all around the world, like you, Mr. Maranovsky."

"Leopold. Would you like lozenge?"

"Oh no thank you. I never eat hard candies."

"Very well," Leopold said, and put one in his mouth.

"Leopold. Yes. That is a lovely name," Ms. Ramsey said, allowing her gaze to rest approvingly on the press secretary of Near Upper Pilasia. The proprietress ran through a short list of house guidelines designed to enable the guests to live in "good and cheerful convenience" with one another. Then she rang another bell, and a young man came to collect Leopold's trunk and take it upstairs to his new room.

Before we left Ms. Ramsey, she singled me out, staring deeply into my eyes for a long moment.

"He looks so familiar," Ms. Ramsey said.

"It is possible that you have seen him,"

Leopold said. "He is New York dog. I am borrowing him for my stay."

"I have known many, many dogs, and this one is special," Ms. Ramsey said.

"Yes, he is particularly calm."

"That too," Ms. Ramsey said. "But clearly very intelligent. He seems to be taking it all in. What is his name?"

Leopold looked momentarily embarrassed.

"To tell truth, I have forgotten," the press secretary said. "I think it begins with *R*."

"Let's call him Rembrandt, then," Ms. Ramsey said. "He has the same soulful, sad eyes as the painter of Rijn."

"Rembrandt it is," Leopold said. "Come on, Rembrandt. Let's get settled."

I paused, hesitant to accept the new moniker.

"I'm not sure he likes it," Leopold said.

"He will," Ms. Ramsey said. "Just say it with a bit more force."

Leopold did, and strange as it was to heed a different name, I decided that it was best to follow. There was much to be learned upstairs.

I WAS NOT WELL AC-quainted with the culture and manners of Near Upper Pilasia but learned several things about one native within five minutes of arriving at our new room (which had been Imogen's for so many months). Leopold was: 1) very fond of highly polished black shoes (his trunk contained a dozen pairs); 2) very fond of bow ties, in a variety of colors and widths; and 3) equipped with a large selection of very sophisticated electronic equipment in addition to a laptop computer. While Leopold busied himself putting away his shoes and hanging his bow ties, I tried to make sense of the electronics. I am no expert on such things, but the proliferation of antennae, satellite dishes and one very expensive-looking shotgun microphone made me conclude that Leopold—as is the case with so many embassy attachés—had a clandestine role in addition to whatever services he provided Near Upper Pilasia as a press secretary. Blinko had already set my mind in this direction with his suggestion that a good number of the boarders were, in fact, agents of some power or another, and Leopold's equipment seemed to confirm it. I imagined there must be a waiting list of foreign agents for a place at Ms. Ramsey's boarding-house.

A great fatigue swept over me, and I remembered SparrowHawk's diagnosis of hypothyroidism. Quack though he was, I was certain he was on to something. I had been trying to ignore my condition, but several times over the last day I had been laid flat by a profound tiredness. It was only the excitement of events (and my fear of Haddy McClay's problematic hands) that had kept me awake with a rush of adrenaline. Now this condition and my Labrador nature's twelve-hour sleep requirement overwhelmed me, and I sprawled on the floor. I hoped that Harry would remember to reschedule that veterinary appointment.

"Tired pup," Leopold said between bars of "The Blue Danube Waltz," which he was humming as he arranged his things in the dresser. "Have good nap. You're already earning your keep."

And so I rested but did so productively, by lying on my back with my four paws in the air. This enabled me a full view of the stars on the ceiling, which I could now examine in the light of day. They were plastic adhesives and looked small and cheap. I was surprised that Ms. Ramsey had not noticed them and prevented Imogen's ongoing work. Perhaps she had tried. I was curious to learn more about how my mistress had been perceived in the seemingly close-knit community of the boardinghouse. How I was to do this would be the challenge. But for now I surveyed the ceiling for some pattern that would have been invisible the night before. At first, nothing stood out, but then I noticed a pencil trace along the farthest edge of the stars. I followed the pencil mark and soon realized that there were dozens across the ceiling. There were even more erasures, where Imogen—I assumed it was my mistress—had tried to eliminate the pencil marks, many of which seemed to have been made with a straightedge. But my observations stalled as my eyelids grew heavier and heavier.

Somewhere in the distance, I heard Leopold sit down at the desk and begin to type. Then there was the sound of electronic equipment being shuffled about and assembled. Wires were plugged into outlets. Dials were adjusted. Antennae and satellite dishes moved about the room. Then my ears closed to the sound of the world around me and I began to dream. I dreamed of Imogen. The room was so suffused with her smell—it was the nearest I had been to my mistress in so many months. The subway encounter was nothing compared to this prolonged olfactory contact. My dreams, usually so abstract, were unusually clear. Imogen was standing above me in the room, looking down at me. She was smiling, but her eyes were narrowed just slightly at the corners, as they did whenever she was a little worried. She stooped to pat my belly and scratch me under the chin.

"Randolph," she said, "you've got to carry us all now. But I know you can. Keep Harry safe. Watch out for friends. Friends can be enemies. And don't forget the stars."

Then I dropped out of the dream into a deeper, blacker sleep. The next thing I knew, my leash, which had never been removed, was being tugged.

"Get up, my friend," Leopold said. "You are quite a sleeper and talker. Barking and whining. If I spoke dog, I would have known all of your secrets. Now, though, it is time for you to really earn keep. We must meet neighbors. We are late for early-afternoon tea. And I am very nervous. I am not so good with most humans as I am with your kind."

Leopold gave my head a good rub and we went downstairs. As we approached the landing on the first floor, I heard the clatter of china, the sound of conversation and the smell of many delectables rising from the ground floor. Leopold paused. I could feel his nervousness in the tight grip he held on my leash and the scent of fear. I sat down and looked up at him. His face was a pale green. His breathing had become rapid, shallow and wheezy.

"No, I don't think I will go down to tea now," Leopold said. "I'll get newspaper and read in room, and perhaps Ms. Ramsey can send something up later."

Action was required if I was to deserve my title as a therapy dog. I began to descend the stairs, and to enforce the sense of necessity, I gave a short whine. I hoped that if he focused on me, it would help him escape from his anxieties. It worked. Leopold steadied himself and followed.

"Ah, but we couldn't deprive you of goodies," Leopold said. At the base of the stairs we turned right and proceeded down the long hallway from which Ms. Ramsey had earlier emerged.

The sounds and smells grew closer, and at the end of the hall we found ourselves in a large room with a long wooden table covered with sunflower place mats. Twelve or so people sat around the table, and from what I could smell— I could not see too far above the table—there was an abundance of lemon-poppy muffins, a freshly baked chocolate cake, roast beef and ham sandwiches and a particularly sharp cheddar. There were also urns of fresh coffee and three kinds of juices: apple, pear and pomegranate. Ms. Ramsey sat at the head of the table. The apron was gone and she wore a high-necked white dress that looked like it had come from Merchant Ivory's *A Room with a View.*

"Rembrandt can go to the sunporch with the other animals if you'd like, Mr. Maranovsky," Ms. Ramsey said.

"Leopold, please," the press secretary said. "If it is all same to you, could Rembrandt remain here with me?"

"Of course, Leopold," Ms. Ramsey said. "Dean Perkins is always with us as well."

Ms. Ramsey gestured at an obese bird perched on the sideboard beside the windows. So inert was the animal that at first I thought it was stuffed. Although its features were distorted by excessive feeding, Dean Perkins was clearly a rainbow lorikeet. At the mention of his name, Dean Perkins spoke.

"I'm sorry, Mr. Ramsey," Dean Perkins said. "I'm sorry, Mr. Ramsey."

Ms. Ramsey nodded and tossed him a piece of lemon-poppy muffin, which the bird snagged out of the air with a flick of his head.

"That is extraordinary name for bird, Ms. Ramsey," Leopold said. "And why—may I ask— does he say, 'I'm sorry, *Mr.* Ramsey'?"

"Dean Perkins was the name of the troglodyte at the university who fired my father," Ms. Ramsey said. "This Dean Perkins is doing the hard work of repentance."

"I see," Leopold said, and we proceeded to the sunporch attached to the end of the dining room, where a large number of cats and dogs and the odd reptile were partaking in their own tea, with surprisingly good manners. It seemed that Ms. Ramsey's powerful vision of tranquility and civility had influenced everyone in the house. All the animals, even the ones (unlike Yours Truly) who operated mainly in their lower natures, were peacefully at work on petits fours and tuna briquettes. Leopold found a plate and assembled a healthy selection of the treats for me, then we returned to the dining room. Ms. Ramsey indicated that he take a seat at the corner so that I could sit beside him. He placed the food on the floor beside me and let my leash drop. I had a robust appetite after my nap and ate with gusto, while retaining an acute reportorial sense of the goings-on above table.

Ms. Ramsey introduced Leopold to the other guests. The woman whom we had seen counting recyclables in the lobby on our first visit was there, as was the poet whom we had stepped over in the entranceway. His name was Abraham Pollop, and when Ms. Ramsey noted this man's proficiency at spoken verse—"a king in the oral tradition of the word"—Mr. Pollop, apparently discomfited by such high praise, let fly a string of profanity that stunned the room, especially Dean Perkins.

"I'm sorry, Mr. Ramsey," the rainbow lorikeet said. "I'm sorry, Mr. Ramsey."

"Language, Mr. Pollop," Ms. Ramsey said. "Language. You've disturbed Dean Perkins."

The proprietress threw the bird another piece of lemon-poppy muffin and continued working her way around the table. Four people stood out at once. Despite the rich and beguiling smells rising up from the tuna briquettes and wafting down to me from the delectables on the table, I detected a great deal of anxiety and deception from these four. Leopold's own anxiety, I sensed, was connected to their presence, and their anxiety was connected to him and one another. The deception was a presence in the nature of each of them, a kind of permanent scent or one that through years of inhabiting and promoting lies had become permanent. Deception has a kind of varnishlike smell—distractingly strong, but, like varnish, ultimately just a cover-up for what lies beneath. I assumed these were the diplomats and/or spies Blinko had suggested.

The four sat scattered among the other guests but seemed far apart.

"It has always been my dream to make this place a welcome mat for all nations," Ms. Ramsey said. "It was Daddy's belief that if humans could only learn about one another and transcend the limits of our individual cultures, so many problems would be solved."

Several of the boarders nodded their heads vigorously. Mr. Pollop, the rhetorically inclined bard, seemed ready to launch another barrage of profanity but instead cut himself a monumental hunk of the cheddar, which he buried in his mouth. The four diplomat/spies stared at the wall. Only Leopold responded to Ms. Ramsey.

"We have saying in Near Upper Pilasia that I think you will find apt, Ms. Ramsey," the press secretary intoned. "It is difficult to translate into English, but I will try: though we in Near Upper Pilasia are above Near Lower Pilasia, we must never think ourselves superior."

"That is very enlightened, Leopold," Ms. Ramsey said.

"Yes, it was spoken by our Philosopher-King Egon prior to his glorious slaughter of entire Near Lower Pilasian army in 1585," Leopold said through a mouth full of roast beef.

One of the diplomat/agents coughed. His name was Ponce. I had missed his last name because I was exploring the layers of my last petit four, but I gathered he was of South American origin and did something culinary at the United Nations.

"Ha," Ponce said. "Lower Pilasia came back to defeat your country a decade later in one of the most legendary routs in military history and Egon lost his head."

Leopold bristled but remained silent.

"Ponce, please, remember the house rule against inflammatory statements," Ms. Ramsey cautioned. "Leopold was merely taking the ideal sentiment of human brotherhood and rescuing it from the sordid march of history."

I had caught the full names of the three other men: Otis Cheng, Max de Tocqueville and Lindmar Wingman (pronounced Wing-en). These men were not as forceful as Ponce, but they were clearly interested in Leopold. They also all seemed to be cut from a similar mold. Their native accents were indistinct. Their pronunciation of English smooth and generic. Their manners schooled and scrupulous, but in a way that struck me as being learned in adulthood rather than in youth. I also had the sense that all five of the men had met one another before and concluded that perhaps the world of international espionage was a smaller one than I had thought.

"Why have you come to New York, Mr. Press Secretary?" Lindmar asked Leopold.

"For conference," Leopold replied.

"Which conference? There are thirty currently ongoing at the United Nations," Max de Tocqueville said. "It isn't, by chance, the Forum on the Exploration of Norms and Standards for Nonrenewable Energy for Developing Nations?"

"Oh no," Leopold said. "We in Near Upper Pilasia have little interest in such things. Nor do we have manpower. We are modest country with modest means in world of giants."

"What are you here for, then?" Otis Cheng asked.

"The Forum for Linguistic Goals for a New

Century," Leopold said. "We in Near Upper Pilasia believe that building language bridges between cultures will someday achieve those noble goals that Ms. Ramsey has articulated and result in true connectedness of our species."

"Isn't that amazing," Ms. Ramsey said. "All five of you are attending the same meeting. The United Nations is so wonderful. That is why I keep places open for those who work for that wonderful institution. Leopold, these four aren't just here for this forum, they are my very honored near-permanent guests. They all arrived together or, at least, within days of one another. I was so pleased. What has it been, Mr. Cheng? A year?"

"Something like that," Mr. Cheng said, tapping his teaspoon on the edge of his coffee cup. "I have enjoyed it greatly. Your hospitality knows no bounds, Ms. Ramsey."

Mr. Cheng was about to say something else, but he was interrupted by events. Three things seemed to occur simultaneously. One of the windows cracked and glass spilled onto the carpet. Dean Perkins, a large piece of lemon-poppy muffin in his beak, squawked and hopped into the air as several of his feathers were separated from his body. And the poet, Abraham Pollop, slumped facefirst into the remains of his roast beef sandwich and large slice of chocolate cake. Then several other things happened in quick succession. Otis Cheng, Max de Tocqueville and Lindmar Wingman rolled onto the floor and crawled for cover. Leopold fainted and slid off his chair. And Ms. Ramsey screamed while the rest of the residents remained stunned and unmoving. A halo of bright red blood spilled over the poet's roast beef and chocolate cake and flowed in all directions across the table, turning the sunflower place mats brown on contact.

"Abraham," the recyclables lady pleaded, nudging the man. "Abraham, wake up."

"He's dead," Max de Tocqueville announced. "The exit wound took off most of his face."

All three men were already back on their feet.

"It was a sniper," de Tocqueville continued. "He is gone now, but he shot from that rooftop over there."

De Tocqueville pointed at a building down the street with a roof garden.

"It was a difficult angle," de Tocqueville said appreciatively. "He must be an expert."

Ms. Ramsey had regained herself and began issuing orders. Abraham Pollop was lain on the floor and emergency resuscitation was attempted, but de Tocqueville's judgment was confirmed. Pollop was quite dead. Within minutes an emergency-services crew had arrived. They moved leisurely. There was no hurry with a corpse. A few minutes after this, Detective Davis arrived.

The room had cleared of all the diners except for Ms. Ramsey, the four diplomat/spies and Leopold, whom the emergency-services crew had revived and moved to a corner of the room. Now he lay with his head on a pillow and his feet up. He refused to be taken to the hospital.

Detective Davis stood over the poet's body.

"What a shame," he said.

"He was a great oral poet," Ms. Ramsey said. "I hope the tradition does not die with him."

"He was also a witness. He saw Imogen flee," Detective Davis observed. "Ms. Ramsey, I am going to need to seal off this room for the next few hours while we remove the body and gather forensic evidence. Afterward, I will want to speak with whomever was present in this room at the time of the shooting. I'm sorry, but it seems like you're getting used to the routine."

The detective walked over to the window and looked out.

De Tocqueville pointed at the rooftop he had indicated to us minutes earlier.

"The shot came from there," de Tocqueville now told the detective.

Detective Davis looked de Tocqueville up and down as if trying to place him. Then he followed the invisible line the man was indicating with his finger above the parked cars and across the street.

"That is quite a shot," Detective Davis said. "And you say you heard only one?"

"We didn't hear any," Ms. Ramsey said. "Just the glass breaking, Dean Perkins—that's the bird—squawking and poor, poor Mr. Pollop falling dead."

"A silencer," Detective Davis murmured. "But still one shot. At least, no one was aware of any others."

"Just the single round," de Tocqueville agreed. "Yes, he was quite a shot."

"He?" Detective Davis said.

Then the police officer asked for the room to be cleared. Leopold was helped to his feet, and as his senses returned so did his anxiety. I had remained near the corner of the table, observing the commotion, and Leopold now approached to reclaim me.

"Whose dog is that?" Detective Davis asked.

"It is mine, Detective," Leopold answered.

"He looks like a dog I know," Detective Davis said.

"Come with us, Rembrandt," Ms. Ramsey said, taking Leopold's arm and leading both of us from the room.

"Dogs are wonderful, aren't they?" Detective Davis observed, the odd sliver of transcendent joy breaking through the grim reality of his job.

Ms. Ramsey paused and took one last look at her dead boarder.

"Indeed they are," Ms. Ramsey said. "They do not shoot guns. Daddy was convinced that they were smarter and kinder than we could ever be."

MANY OF THE BOARDERS had congregated in the lobby, much the way I imagine they did on the night when Harry had arrived to find Detective Davis and receive the news that his missing love was suspected of murder. Ms. Ramsey moved among them, offering food and drink.

"The best response to shock is to stay well fed and well hydrated. Daddy used to say drink plenty of liquids in times of stress," Ms. Ramsey said as she handed the woman with the recyclables a donut and a large glass of lemonade, which she had secured from the kitchen before the forensics team arrived and declared it off limits.

"It is so, so terrible," the woman with the recyclables moaned as tears ran down her nose and into her lemonade. "He was very gifted."

"He was just an old drunk," a man muttered. I recognized him as one of the two men who had stepped around Abraham Pollop when he lay in the lobby the previous day.

"We all have our demons," Ms. Ramsey said. "No one deserves such a fate, and on the sunflower place mats. What a tragedy."

Leopold sighed. Color was gradually returning to his face. The four diplomat/spies were nowhere to be seen, and the crowd in the lobby was going in endless circles of speculation. The general consensus seemed to be that it was a random act, one of those bizarre urban occurrences that claim the occasional life. And even though the boarders were initially afraid for their own lives, soon—as is the human way once danger seems to have passed—a kind of normalcy returned. Abraham Pollop was the sacrifice to death and no other victims were immediately required. Death's appetite had been sated. I was doubtful of this. If anything, death's appetite was growing.

Leopold turned to go out the door, but Ms. Ramsey stopped him.

"Mr. Maranovsky, I don't think you should leave. I am so sorry for this terrible turn of events on your first day with us, but the detective explicitly said that he wants all the people who were in the dining room at the time of Mr. Pollop's demise to stay put. I think he will be interviewing everyone. That is what he did last time."

"There was last time?" Leopold asked.

"Oh yes, we have had more than our share of worries recently," Ms. Ramsey said, and busied herself in her office before my temporary master could pose a follow-up question.

Leopold sighed again, and we began to weave our way upstairs past two men seated on the bottom steps, dressed as women and speaking in self-conscious *Cage aux Folles* fashion. But just as we reached the top of the first flight, Detective Davis entered the lobby and stopped us.

"Excuse me," he said, addressing the room and trying to be heard above the noise of several different conversations. "If you don't mind, I need a moment of your time. Anyone who was in the dining room when the victim was killed, I'd like to speak with you now. We'll try to be as orderly as possible and take as little of your time as possible. I know it's been a sad day for all of you. Forensics is still at work, so I'd like to see each of you, individually, in the kitchen."

Leopold continued to climb the stairs.

"Sir, if you don't mind, I'd like to start with you," Detective Davis called after him.

We arrived in the kitchen. It was a surprisingly tiny space, given Ms. Ramsey's endless supply line of food. Detective Davis was eating a lemon–poppy seed muffin, drinking a cup of coffee and looking at a black sniper rifle. He motioned to a chair pushed up against the two-burner stove.

"Is that murder weapon?" Leopold asked.

"We believe so," Detective Davis said. "It was fired once and then discarded."

"So Frenchman was right," Leopold asked.

"Is that what he is?" Detective Davis said. "It's hard to tell—it's the United Nations around here."

"Yes, Ms. Ramsey keeps rooms available for diplomatic attachés and the like," Leopold said. "In fact, technically I'm not required to speak with you."

"I'm aware of that, Mr. . . . ."

"Mr. Maranovsky. I am rotating press secretary for Near Upper Pilasia. You can call me Leopold."

"I'm aware of that, Leopold, and speaking on behalf of the New York City Police Department, we appreciate your cooperation."

"May I ask what you think has gone on here? Are we in any danger? That is very sophisticated-looking gun."

For all of my temporary master's seeming softness, there was a savvy worldliness right beneath the surface, quite used to things like guns and assassination.

"It is a very sophisticated gun," Detective Davis said. "It is Heckler and Koch PSG-1—one of the most highly regarded short-range urban sniper rifles in the world. This one's been equipped with a sight worth tens of thousands of dollars and a state-of-the-art sound muffler. It certainly explains how the shooter was able to make the kill. What doesn't make sense is why the gun would have been left on a rooftop of an empty building. And even if the gun couldn't be disassembled and needed to be left, why not take the sight and the muffler?"

"This is all Greek to me, as you Americans say," Leopold said. "I am chiefly interested in linguistics, not guns and death. We Near Upper Pilasians are peaceful people. From what little I witnessed at tea table, this poet was foul-mouthed and I doubt possessed much in way of literary merit, but he did not deserve to die. Alas, *the moving finger writes and, having writ, moves on. Not all your piety nor wit shall lure it back to cancel half a line. Nor all your tears wash out a word of it.*"

Detective Davis shrugged, apparently not

recognizing the reference to the poetic quatrain of the *Rubaiyat of Omar Khayyam*—any fatalist's favorite, since it speaks of the brutal power of time and events to break the strongest of hopes and wills.

"As I said, I appreciate your cooperation and I won't take too much of your time," Detective Davis said. "Ms. Ramsey said you've just arrived."

"Yes, I'm in town for United Nations conference."

"A tough thing to arrive to," Detective Davis said. "Can you describe how it happened?"

"Yes, we were eating around table and poor fellow dropped dead in his chocolate cake."

"Do you remember what you were talking about?" Detective Davis said.

"No, Detective, I'm afraid I don't," Leopold said. "Wait a moment: we were speaking about how long one of boarders—Asian man—had been living here. Then window cracked, bird squawked and, as I've mentioned, poet dropped into chocolate cake."

"Did you notice who was sitting next to the poet?" Detective Davis asked.

"A funny little woman with enormous bag of cans and bottles sat to his right, and chair to his left was empty."

Detective Davis furrowed his brow.

"The backs of those chairs are pretty high, aren't they?"

"Yes, they're unusual chairs."

"But the poet was a tall man, so his head was well above the back? It cleared it by several inches?"

"I suppose it would have, Detective," Leopold said.

"Do you know whether he usually sat there?" Detective Davis asked.

"As you yourself said, Detective, I have only just arrived. I am not familiar with customs of house yet," Leopold said. I detected a slight uptick in his anxiety through both his scent and the heel of his highly polished black shoe, which he pressed back into the floor.

"So seating was casual," Detective Davis continued.

"It seems."

"Well, that's about it, Leopold," Detective Davis said.

"May I ask again? What do you think has gone on here? And are we in any danger?"

Detective Davis looked out the window.

"It's an almost philosophical question. Almost a spiritual question. The world is on fire," the policeman said, revealing his roots as a

Buddhist monk. "I guess we are always in danger from something, but in terms of a specific threat to you or most of the residents of this boardinghouse from a high-caliber, hollow-point nine-mm round—nope, the chances are very good that you're safe. This was a specific killing. Someone wanted Abraham Pollop dead. They could have killed anyone or everyone else in the room, but they didn't. They chose him and they put him down."

"So it was professional job, as they say?"

"I'm not sure of that," Detective Davis said. "These rifles and that sight could be used fairly effectively by almost anyone. It's user-friendly—not that it's in most people's price range."

"So Frenchman is wrong about it being difficult shot?"

"No. It was difficult. It just wasn't that difficult," Detective Davis said.

Leopold began to move toward the door.

"One last thing, Mr. Maranovsky. Did you happen to notice anyone make any particular gestures before Pollop was killed?"

"Gesture? What do you mean, Detective?"

"Something that could be interpreted as pointing out Pollop to the shooter?"

Leopold paused. I could remember no such gesture, but my view of the table was partially impeded by the height and angle. But my temporary master apparently was trying hard to remember, so hard that in the end he made something up—he began to reek of deceit (a terrible smell, as I've suggested).

"Now that you mention it, I did," Leopold said, dropping his voice to a confidential hush. "What I tell you is strictly for your ears, yes, Detective?"

Detective Davis nodded.

"Both Asian and Frenchman did things with their utensils that could be interpreted in this way. The Asian seemed to point his coffee spoon subtly but like compass needle in poor man's direction, and Frenchman did same with his butter knife."

I could not attest to what de Tocqueville had done with his utensil, but I clearly remember that while Otis Cheng tapped his saucer with his coffee spoon, he did not point it at anyone. Leopold seemed to want to muddy the waters for his diplomatic peers.

"Interesting," Detective Davis said. "I will be speaking with them."

"But you will not mention this," Leopold said.

"I will not mention that *you* said this," Detective Davis assured him.

A young police officer entered the room, holding a piece of paper.

"There were no prints on the gun, Detective Davis," he reported. "But we've run a mobile DNA test on the hair in the firing mechanism and..."

The young man paused as if for dramatic effect.

"We're not on some New York police show, Jim," Detective Davis said. "Who is it?"

"It's Imogen. She's our shooter."

I couldn't believe the name I heard. How could this be true? Not only did I refuse to believe that my mistress was a killer, I knew she despised firearms (Harry had received his grandfather Oswald's World War II–era .45 only after she disappeared—the gun would have been an unfathomable possession in a house shared with Imogen). Detective Davis did not readily accept the news either. For the first time in my acquaintance with him, I noticed him lose his color—albeit only slightly. But he responded to his colleague in a measured and educational fashion.

"Jim, you have to observe the way you think. You are saying two separate things: one, you found a certain person's DNA on the murder weapon, or at least what we believe at this moment—three-forty-seven on a Wednesday afternoon—is the murder weapon, and, two, that she is the shooter because of this presence of DNA. The trick is to keep them separate in your mind until it becomes absolutely clear that the facts are not separate at all but lead to the same conclusion. Our calling is about building evidence until we reach this point. As we build, there is no point to jump ahead."

"Right, sir, but I think it's still pretty much a slam dunk," the young detective said.

Detective Davis shrugged. "There is no such thing as a slam dunk anywhere off the basketball court," he said. "I'm sorry, Mr. Maranovsky. You can leave now. Thank you."

Leopold bowed and we left the room. As we passed the entrance to the dining room, I saw that all the sunflower place mats had been collected and sealed into clear-plastic evidence bags, and a technician was in the process of removing a small bright metal object from a lemon–poppy seed muffin with a pair of tweezers.

"Got it," he said, as the tweezers came free. He held the object up to the light.

It was a bullet.

The crowd in the lobby had thinned. Those who remained had grown quiet, as if the reality of the situation had settled in about them like a cold fog. The four diplomat/spies were present, as were the other occupants of the table. Ms. Ramsey was still moving among her "guests" but much slower than before. Leopold passed through the room with a nod, and as we mounted the stairs to our room, the stretcher carrying the oral poet's body passed through the lobby and out the door to the coroner's wagon waiting on the street.

"Can you imagine," Ms. Ramsey observed softly. "When poor Abraham walked into the dining room, he did not know that he would be carried out dead."

Then the stalwart proprietress sank into the overstuffed cushions of one of the sofas and began to sob. But in a muffled, discreet sort of way.

Each step up the stairs was a struggle for me. My fatigue seemed to have gotten worse despite my long nap earlier that day. When we reached our room, I curled up next to the bed. Leopold settled in at his desk and began tapping away on the laptop. I fell into another sleep. This time, though, my dreams were a chaos of terrible images. From a dark stage, Mr. Pollop delivered an obscenity-laced poem on sudden death. He sipped from a glass of thick red pomegranate juice, but, instead of having his thirst quenched, his mouth only became drier and drier. In a rage he hissed his lines, until his tongue cleaved and he could no longer speak at all. Then a second spotlight appeared on the dark stage and Imogen approached the podium, wearing her bright red party dress and carrying a silver platter with a beautifully shaped lemon–poppy seed muffin. She offered the delectable to the poet, and as she did I awoke with a low whine.

"Chasing rabbits?" Leopold asked. "It's alright, boy."

I turned onto my back. The meaning of the dream was painfully obvious. Pomegranate juice, after all, was what Hades, the Greek god of the Underworld, gave to Persephone to bring her down to the land of death. Whatever art was on our poet's foul-mouthed tongue would stay there, and Imogen's troubles were grave indeed. Through half-opened eyes I scanned the dots on the ceiling for some message and, still drowsy, I made connections where there were none. One cluster formed a *G,* another a *U,* another an *I,* and so forth, until the word was spelled: *GUILTY.* I shook sleep off and the word disappeared into the meaningless jumble of stars.

"It is time to get ready for banquet, my friend," Leopold said, getting up from the desk and rubbing my belly with his foot. "Tonight you will earn your keep. There is formal diplomatic gala at headquarters of United Nations to inaugurate our weeklong linguistics conference. You must keep me very calm. Though I am experienced in these matters of state, I am still—somewhere deep inside—only little Leo from the tiny village of Moot in Near Upper Pilasia, easily flustered by speed and manners of modern world. First, nice long shower."

The pudgy diplomat took a fresh towel folded on the end of the bed and disappeared down the hall to the shower. My head spun and I felt quite groggy, but I hopped up onto the desk chair and examined the laptop. To my surprise, my temporary master had left the device powered up and still connected to the Internet. I hoped his shower would be long, since I wanted to compose my first message to Harry from my new e-mail account. It was not that I had anything specific to report. He would learn soon enough through other channels of that day's murder and Imogen's suspected role, but perhaps I could reestablish a bridge to him that would support him as he went forward. I knew from his conversation with Blinko that Harry would be visiting the boardinghouse frequently and use my cover as a therapy dog to try to discover who really murdered the young man beneath the parachute. Communicating by e-mail would give us a direct line of communication about things only I could learn.

Leopold's laptop had a pointing device, which was difficult to manipulate with my snout. Just as I was about to navigate to my e-mail account, my nose slipped and suddenly I found myself in an entirely different place, a magical place, an extraordinarily wonderful place. Somehow I had stumbled upon an online bookstore. With a few more snout strokes and keypad jabs, I made my way to a specific screen where, floating on the screen in near three-dimensionality, I found *The Inferno of Dante* (the Pinsky translation). As I have mentioned, our copy was still under the daybed in the living room, with little hope of salvage. Not only was the Dante for sale, but it had been paired with a second title that I longed to read, Joyce's *Ulysses* (I had devoured his *Dubliners* and *A Portrait of the Artist as a Young Man*, courtesy of Imogen's college collection). For a substantial discount a purchaser could get both books and a tote bag with Virginia Woolf's profile emblazoned on both sides. Not since my encounter with the bewitching sidewalk pâté of Central Park West had I experienced such a sense of transcendence (in fact, I had the sudden urge to roll). A dog—as you have likely gathered—is given to more moments of this kind of escape than a human, moments when we seem lifted off our four legs and beyond the confines of our limited bodies and thrust into the glorious hurly-burly of life and living. These are the moments when most dogs race around the kitchen table or jump into the pool. Typically, my rational mind keeps these moments to a minimum, but when they occur I am powerless to resist.

Lost in the moment, I added the two books (and the complimentary tote bag) to my shopping cart and, putting aside any ethical concerns, I hurriedly entered Harry's credit-card number—which I easily recalled from the many times he had spoken it aloud when ordering food delivery. Then I typed in our address on 90th Street and selected *Priority Delivery*. My dog's life had known only dependency: dependency on my owner for walks and food and a general dependency on human society to continue to find my kind useful or lovable. Online shopping was a kind of empowerment, and it was also—sad to say—a comfort in the face of the gruesome death in the dining room.

I heard a door down the hallway open and

shut and Leopold's feet coming down the hall. I closed the screen with the books and hopped back onto the floor. When he entered, I delivered a look of doe-eyed innocence that generally earns a pat and a biscuit if one is on hand.

"What good guard dog," Leopold said. He shut the door behind him and removed a tuxedo shirt from a hanger in the closet.

He whistled "Blue Danube" as he dressed and I curled up at the base of the bed, warmed by the excitement of my recent purchase. I could not wait for my books and complimentary tote bag to arrive.

A DANGEROUS MAN DELIVERS
A TOOTHBRUSH

CRISIS AT THE UNITED NATIONS
DOG RUN

JUST AS YOURS TRULY began to recognize that he had once again been less than noble and loyal in his behavior, there was a knock on the door. Leopold, dressed only in shirttails and with what remained of his hair still in need of combing, opened it without hesitation.

Ponce, the diplomat/spy of vague South American origin, stood in the doorway, pointing a blunt object at Leopold.

"Here's the toothbrush you needed," Ponce said.

"Come in," Leopold said, and in classic Hollywood cloak-and-dagger fashion poked his pudgy face into the hallway to determine whether there was anyone following Ponce. Determining that there was not, he closed the door. Ponce sat down on the bed.

"I'm not an amateur, Leopold," Ponce said.

Leopold gave a short apologetic bow.

"I am getting bit ridiculous in my old age, Ponce," Leopold said.

"Why the dog?"

"Ah, I am bundle of nerves. Dogs, it seems, are only cure. I have tried all manner of sedatives, but they dull me bit too much for our sensitive line of work."

"A shame about the poet," Ponce said casually, as if a man were shot over tea every day.

"Are you sure it wasn't meant for one of us?"

Ponce shrugged.

"I can't believe that you fainted," Ponce said.

"It was humiliating but effective," Leopold said, examining the knot of his bow tie in the mirror. "The detective could hardly be bothered with me."

"I threatened him with diplomatic immunity," Ponce said.

"Why?"

"Because I can."

"You always were hothead," Leopold said, as if he hadn't done almost the same thing himself. "And that idiotic Frenchman..."

"De Tocqueville is Swiss," Ponce corrected.

"Talking like he was military expert right out of gate."

"I thought you fainted."

"It was light faint."

"You are a tricky one," Ponce said. "Strange that you showed up today of all days."

"A coincidence and damn nuisance. Of course, Home Office won't be pleased. They don't like our people being near anything that might become media event."

"This won't," Ponce said confidently. "They've already quashed it at the highest levels."

"Yes?"

"I got advance word that this won't be going anywhere," Ponce said. "And when I was speaking with the detective, a representative from some government agency arrived and had a few choice words for the lieutenant. After that his tone was quite different. Defeat had crept in. Not that he seemed to be on to anything."

"What have you boys been up to?" Leopold asked. "Two murders in a week. If Near Upper Pilasia were playing, I'd be furious. Six months spent trying to secure rights to reserve, and then violence and empty hands. What farce."

"I have never met a more clever woman than Imogen," Ponce said. "Nor a more elegant one."

"You sound like you are in love," Leopold said. He was now entirely clothed in his evening attire.

"She is a woman worthy of being loved,"

Ponce said in a voice that was free of his usual dose of cynicism and world-weariness.

"I think she played you all and now she is gone and none of you has what you wanted. Even major players were fooled on this one. Otis Cheng and his lot have been left with nothing."

"Of course, Near Upper Pilasia isn't interested in the outcome at all," Ponce said.

"Only in entertainment value," Leopold said. "We have never been ones to get into Great Game. Oh yes, in old days we subcontracted for major players, but now we are happy with scraps that fall from table. As I said, I am here for linguistics conference."

"If you are, then you are the only one."

"My question is why?" Leopold mused, sitting down at the desk and giving me another belly rub with his foot.

"You mean, why has someone framed her," Ponce said.

"Indeed. Clearly she is not murderer, and this was wet operation. But by killing witness who implicated Imogen, it only makes her look more guilty. It makes no sense."

"So you do know more about the case," Ponce said.

"I like to keep abreast of current events, and

this maneuver confuses me. What is to be gained by turning her into suspect? If she is apprehended, then she loses all value because she loses claim to resource. She will be disinherited, no? If she is not arrested, then she might retain claim, but she cannot inherit it unless she is cleared. But *if* she is cleared, then real killer will be compromised—which will presumably involve turning in trained member of one's team. It makes no sense."

"This is deep play," Ponce said. "It wasn't us— I'm sure you'd like to know. Professional courtesy permits me to tell you that much and also deliver a toothbrush. Do you really need it, by the way?"

"Actually, I do. Those damn poppy seeds get stuck in every crack and crevice," Leopold said, taking the implement. "Of all the things to forget to pack. So it wasn't you? Do you think it was Cheng? De Tocqueville?"

"I could not say," Ponce said. "But it was one of them or an operative—and my sense is that they would not have done it themselves. All of us were in the final stages of our operations. It was frustrating, but there seemed to be movement— and it was fair. But someone wanted to change the rules, I think. They got tired of Imogen playing Holly Golightly. They wanted a forced marriage."

"Good luck to them," Leopold said. "But this simply wasn't done in old days."

"Things are more desperate now," Ponce said. "The resource is valuable and the need is great. There is a scramble on for raw materials and energy. I wouldn't be surprised if it all ends in a global war."

"Let's hope not. Things have been desperate before," Leopold said. "As long as we have United Nations and dear, daffy Ms. Ramsey and all useful players flitting about in shadows, things should not derail. You are young yet, Ponce. I've seen it cycle around several times now."

"So it can keep going like this?" Ponce asked. For a moment he sounded like a student.

"*When everyone is dead Great Game is finished. Not before,*" Leopold said, without mentioning that the pithy statement came from Rudyard Kipling's novel *Kim*.

"Well, I've got to go," Ponce said. "I'm taking an adult-education class at the Learning Center."

"Really?" Leopold asked. "What about?"

"They've got two lectures on. It'll either be

Buying Your First Home at Foreclosure or Designing the Perfect Gift Basket."

"Fascinating," Leopold said. "It is good to hear that you have outside interests. You will need that if you wish to be in this business for long haul. Thank you for toothbrush."

Ponce nodded and left after Leopold had taken his usual precaution of checking the hallway. Then Leopold looked at his watch.

"We must go or we'll miss cocktails," he said.

I would not have time to reflect upon all of the extraordinary things that I had just heard. Blinko seemed right. The boardinghouse was a hotbed of spies and agents, all engaged in trying to gain rights to the fortune—"resource," they had called it—that would soon belong to my mistress by law. The casualness of the two men surprised me, but perhaps it should not have. After all, every profession I have ever encountered has its casual, workaday side. Man seems inclined to be "normal" even in the most abnormal occupations. Leopold and Ponce were no exception. The world might hang in the balance, but there was always the need for a toothbrush or a lecture on the Perfect Gift Basket to put things in some kind of perspective.

Leopold hurried me downstairs. The lobby was deserted and the police were gone. When we reached 5th Street, he hailed a taxi. The driver did not object to my presence. Traffic was light on First Avenue and we were at the United Nations in ten minutes.

"Oh no," Leopold said when we stepped from the vehicle. "You will need to be walked."

My little island is remarkable for many things, not the least of which is the millions of dollars' worth of real estate given over to the recreation of its canine noncitizens. Ah, the dog run. I am not a social creature by nature and would rather curl up with my own thoughts than interact with another dog. Nevertheless, the dog run is a welcome place because of its role in the accomplishment of my Numbers and for entertainment value. Prior to Leopold, my experience with dog runs had been limited to the Bull Moose and a few others. Nothing in those places could have prepared me for what I was to encounter at the dog run adjacent to the United Nations complex. As we passed through a series of four gates to gain entrance, a sign identified the space as the *Dag Hammarskjöld World Pet Unity Area*. There was a second sign written in a dozen languages and tiny print that outlined the exclusion of cats, ferrets and venomous animals as well as pointing out several key behaviors (for the human owners) that would ensure utmost cooperation and goodwill within the dusty pen surrounded by a chain-link fence.

"This is where secretary general brings Flowers and Puppet," Leopold noted as he struggled to open the last gate.

Then he bent down to unhook my leash.

"Be gentle if you see them, Rembrandt. Puppet is recovering from hernia surgery and Flowers is paranoid."

But Puppet and Flowers were nowhere in sight, and my first aim was to navigate across the dog run unscathed. I had spotted a discreet location for a Number 2 on the opposite side behind a bronze statue of Winston Churchill, which was mercifully bottom-heavy and provided good cover for a *Foliage-Finder*. The more diminutive Mahatma Gandhi on the near side was insufficient. Though I admire him, the vegetarian ascetic was no match for the whiskey-guzzling carnivore prime minister's bulk. Unfortunately, several large animals from the Icelandic legation were menacing the yard. There are times when having a generous belly insulates one from the indignity of dog power politics. The Icelandic horde bypassed me but targeted a Yorkie playing with a small orange ball. Soon they had surrounded him. His flustered owner, a striking

African man in a multicolored full-length gown, swept across the space, yelling at the pack, which utterly disregarded him. Fortunately, a Polish Tatra sheepdog—one of the largest specimens I had ever seen, a brute upward of 150 pounds—took up the Yorkie's cause. Falling into rather typical instinctual behavior, he began to growl and herd the Icelandic horde into the base of the Gandhi statue. The Yorkie was picked up by its owner and peace was momentarily restored. I took the opportunity to saunter across to Churchill. Leopold followed, bag in hand, and disposed of the Number 2 with an elegance that complemented his tuxedo-clad persona. A few well-tailored yards of cloth had turned him into a sleek international figure.

In all my observations of humankind, this question of clothing's transformative power stands out. How many people go into debt buying clothes? How many pairs of shoes are really necessary? But still humans seem obsessed with clothes. Many fine thinkers have weighed in on the question and caught up, I suspect, in romantic overexuberance have leaned toward nudism (though it is doubtful that they practiced it themselves). The novelist Katherine Mansfield observed this about clothing: *How idiotic civilization is! Why be given a body if you have to keep it shut up in a case like a rare, rare fiddle!* And Mark Twain offered: *Indecency, vulgarity, obscenity— these are strictly confined to man; he invented them. Among the higher animals there is no trace of them. They hide nothing; they are not ashamed.* Perhaps, Mr. Twain, this does apply to most "higher animals," but we are clothed, after all, in our own fashion and by our own fabric—and even so there are *Foliage-Finders* among my kind and *Phantom-Dumpers,* who do their business without ever being seen. No, I think Montaigne, the father of the essay, is closest to the mark on the human-clothing question: *Man is the sole animal whose nudities offend his own companions, and the only one who, in his natural actions, withdraws and hides himself from his own kind.* As noted, I am always dressed in fashionable black. While a dog's body can be fat or skinny, it can rarely be strange, distorted or grotesque. There are natural limits to how odd we can look. Not so with human beings. Leopold Maranovsky, fresh from showering and minus a towel, presented a very different picture from Leopold Maranovsky, sleek and elegant in an expensive tuxedo. I, for one, applaud the invention of human clothing. May the Churchills, Gandhis and Leopolds of the world long embrace the practice.

After Leopold had disposed of my business,

he reattached my leash and together we left the dog run. As we walked away, the Icelandic pack had resumed their harassment. This time they were left unchecked by the Polish Tatra, who was canoodling with an Irish wolfhound in the shade of a ginkgo tree.

"Damn," Leopold said, looking down at his shoe. He had stepped in the rogue Number 2 of another dog. "People who do not pick up after their animals are barbarians."

He scuffed off the offending matter on the stones, and we hurried along beneath a long line of flagpoles and onto a wide stone pavilion. I suddenly felt very privileged to be entering this legendary institution. The sordid realities of power politics aside, somewhere contained within the United Nations complex was an enlivening and liberating ideal, and sometimes idealism is one's only defense in dark times. Peace and freedom are ideals for which Yours Truly will always be willing to make a fool out of himself.

Leopold flashed an identification badge, and we were whisked by a guard past the creeping line of tourists waiting to pass through the metal detectors for a glimpse of the General Assembly. Even so, we were subjected to a metal detector, both of us were given pat-downs and my collar was removed and put into a bomb-sniffing machine.

"Gentlemen, gentlemen," Leopold protested. "My dog is not bomb."

The guards only nodded, and put the leash into the machine as well.

When this was over, we walked across the monumental lobby, ascended two escalators and arrived in a ballroom filled with people in evening wear. There was much laughter, the occasional hushed tones of shared confidence and the light clatter of glasses and plates heavy with hors d'oeuvres.

I could sense Leopold's anxiety growing with each step until, only a few feet inside the room, he froze. My tail gave an encouraging wag. When this didn't work, I sat down next to him, allowing my generous Labrador girth to lean against his right leg. Cynics might see this maneuver as a pathetic bid for food, and given the urgencies of a Lab's stomach this could sometimes be true, but at this moment it was my best way of reminding my charge that I was there to support him. Leopold noticed, bent down and patted me.

"How are you doing, boy?" Leopold asked, and as if this act of reaching out and the sound of his own voice had steadied him, he rose to his feet and proceeded to the bar to get a cocktail.

"A Manhattan," Leopold said to the bartender in a moderately steady voice. He was still in a state of near panic even after the first few sips of his beverage, so I directed him to a cozy spot along the wall from which he could gather his strength and we could both survey the room.

Ponce's words had made me expect to see a place teeming with diplomat/spies, a virtual cavalcade of cloak-and-dagger types using "professional courtesy" in intricate plays for the upper hand. Of course, in the real world things are rarely so obvious or so interesting. The diplomat/spy is the aging academic or the bespectacled tax accountant behaving bureaucratically even where death and extortion are involved. A poster board at the ballroom's entrance had welcomed all comers to something called *A Night of Linguistics*. If any of the occupants of the room were interested in anything but the stated subject, I could not tell. None of the four diplomat/spies from the boardinghouse was present. I began to believe that Leopold was likely here for the cocktails and the free meal even if it meant putting his anxiety to the test. Leopold, like Yours Truly, seemed to understand the value of the stomach.

Leopold polished off two more Manhattans before everyone was ushered into an adjoining dining room. Dinner passed amid a din of academic gossip. Leopold had little to contribute and didn't seem to know any of the people at the table. He ate his filet mignon, baby carrots and whipped potatoes with vigor and in silence and sucked down great quantities of Bulgarian red wine. From time to time he noticed—to my embarrassment but also relief—that I was drooling and delivered a few choice pieces of the beef below table.

"This is a very conventional meal for the United Nations kitchen," one of our table companions complained. "Typically, the fare is much more wide-reaching and representative. I cannot even remember all of the delicacies at the End Global Hunger Dinner last week. Needless to say, we all stuffed ourselves silly."

Memories of that fine meal did not prevent him from cramming a heaping forkful of beef into his mouth as he continued to speak.

"Even the staff cafeteria downstairs is filled with the most unique specialties from around the world. Once I actually saw Near Upper Pilasian goats' ears in jellied blood among the sushi and yogurts."

Leopold winced.

"That is savage delicacy and bastardized import from Near *Lower* Pilasia," the press secretary growled. "If I had kopek for every time some idiotnik made mistake about goat ear, I would be wealthy man."

Leopold's undiplomatic response did not deter his table companion.

"I apologize for any offense, but goats' ears are most certainly a Near Upper Pilasian delicacy," the man insisted. "But that's beside the point. I was merely saying that the kitchen staff at the United Nations is extraordinary and constantly pushing the limits of our culinary prison to include all of the edible wonders of the world."

Leopold drained his wineglass and motioned to the waiter for a refill, which he immediately lifted to his lips. I had thought that Harry was a robust drinker, but the press secretary from Near Upper Pilasia had a monumental capacity. Before I could reflect on human drunkenness (for which I would have referred to Rabelais), a woman with a clipboard addressed the crowd from the dais at the front of the room, and a screen began to lower behind her.

"Ah, the keynote presentation with diagrams. Wonderful," the man said. "I am so eager to hear Professor Kretchmar's insights into the idioms of the Mati Mati tribe of the Amazon tributaries."

"God help us," Leopold grunted. I half expected him to leap to his feet, but instead his
multitiered chin dropped to his chest and he began to snore.

Having an active interest in almost all areas of
academic inquiry, Yours Truly listened with genuine enthusiasm to the lecture. But as the idioms of the Mati Mati tribe were dissected by
the keynote speaker, a great and irresistible fatigue again descended over me and soon I too
was fast asleep on the banquet-hall floor.

THE NEXT DAY LEOPOLD awoke with the dawn. Yours Truly could have slept until noon, but the press secretary insisted on rising for breakfast. We had managed to find our way home despite the late hour and my temporary master's extreme inebriation. Ms. Ramsey had been awake when Leopold stumbled home, and she informed him that Harry had stopped by to "check up on things." I suspected he was following Blinko's advice and using my presence at the boardinghouse as a pretense to visit often. Ms. Ramsey also mentioned that Harry had left word about a vet appointment rescheduled for the morning, but Leopold had not paid much attention.

This was unfortunate, because now my head spun and my body was heavy, a sensation that seemed to have become permanent. I remained stretched in a warm sliver of sunlight as Leopold moved about the small room, getting ready for the day. He checked his e-mails. Seeing him do this, I knew that I should feel an urgency to communicate with Harry, but I didn't.

The halls were empty when we left the room and began to make our way downstairs. Extra-ordinary aromas were wafting upstairs from the kitchen: bacon and home fries, eggs and pan-cakes, banana bread. I took a deep snout sample and momentarily felt the heaviness lift from my bones. Thus distracted, I did not immediately notice another smell beneath the cooking as we approached the second landing. Alas, it was a smell that I had become all too familiar with in recent months: death.

Leopold was about to proceed down the stairs to the lobby when I pulled him up.

"Rembrandt," Leopold said. "Come, boy. Breakfast is waiting."

But the smell was potent and fresh and com-ing from around the corner and down the hall-way. It was an imperative smell. A smell that demanded action. I began pulling the press sec-retary toward it. At first he resisted, but I was insistent and he relented. When we rounded the corner, we saw her slumped at the end of the corridor beneath a window with red-and-white farmhouse curtains.

"Oh my," Leopold said, stopping us while we were some twenty feet distant.

The recyclables lady's corpse seemed peaceful, but her face was distorted by a twenty-ounce bottle of soda that had been crammed into her mouth base-first, with the neck and mouth pointing upward at a sharp angle to the ceiling. The effect was to make her head look like a grotesque fountain spout. Her large clear-plastic bag of recyclables was beside her body on the floor, and her left arm was draped over it as if she were posing for a photograph with a good friend.

"Quite terrible," Leopold observed. "She was only stupid, innocent woman. This is *not* done."

The diplomat/spy did not move any closer, but I knew that I must. As distasteful as it was, it was critical that I perform a full snout stamp on the poor woman. If, as I suspected, one of the people in the house was responsible, then I would know. I gave a heave forward and pulled my leash from Leopold's hand.

"Rembrandt, no," Leopold shouted. Even the most casual observer of dogs will recognize the snout stamp. A dog approaches the leg of a human and nudges his or her nose into the calf or shin. This is the snout stamp. In normal situations the snout stamp serves two purposes: it gives the dog all the identifying scents of that person, and it leaves a trace of the dog's own scent as an easy way to identify that human in the future. It is more discreet than marking them with that other leg-lifting behavior and certainly more hygienic. But since the recyclables lady would sadly be on her way to the city morgue and points beyond, I needed only to retrieve scent, not leave a mark. In a moment I was done and had already begun to back away from the corpse when Leopold picked up my leash and gave a sharp yank.

"Bad dog," Leopold said. "Very bad dog."

The commotion had awoken several of the boarders and they now appeared in the hallway, in various states of undress. A scream went up from a female impersonator and soon Ms. Ramsey had arrived, puffing up the stairs with a spatula in hand that glistened with bacon grease.

"Rembrandt found her," Leopold said. "I believe she is dead."

"Oh no," Ms. Ramsey said. "Not again. Sweet Miss Dunbar and all her cans and bottles. Just last night she told me she was going to finally redeem them. All of them. They had gotten so heavy for her. She would have been free."

"She's free now," Leopold said.

One of the boarders, a large man wearing overalls and a hard hat, took Ms. Ramsey in his arms just as the proprietress was about to faint. The female impersonator inched toward the body.

"My God, she's been skewered," the female impersonator said.

In my hurry to perform my snout stamp, I had missed the apparent cause of death: a long metal skewer protruded from Miss Dunbar's chest, as if she were a kabob.

"And what's she holding?" another boarder asked. After the initial shock of discovering the body, everyone had grown bolder, and the boarders now formed a semicircle around the body.

"It looks like jewelry," the female impersonator said. Indeed, it was jewelry, and with a spirit of near despair I was prepared to recognize it as some kitschy icon from Imogen's collection, but it wasn't. Instead, it was a small lapis lazuli stone in a simple metal housing with a clasp that suggested it was meant to be connected to a necklace.

"Tasteless," the female impersonator declared. *But not kitsch, per se,* I thought.

Soon the police arrived, and Detective Davis was looking more beleaguered than I had ever seen him. Ms. Ramsey attempted to distract the house with breakfast, declaring it a "two-egg day if there ever was one." With the exception of Leopold, whose appetite seemed unaffected by events, the boarders picked at their breakfasts. Detective Davis appeared downstairs and again spoke with the boarders individually, but this time he held his investigations in a corner of the lobby, since the kitchen and dining room were busy. Leopold went first and related how he had found Miss Dunbar, but I could tell Detective Davis—while always the professional—felt constrained by something. His scent was strong with frustration and annoyance. Apparently Ponce was right and Detective Davis had been hamstrung in his detective work by higher authorities. At one point the frustration seemed to come to the surface in a surprising exchange.

"Tell me, Mr. Maranovsky, aren't you the least bit surprised by any of this?" Detective Davis said. "After all, you've been here two days and two people have died. Does this usually happen when you visit New York?"

"You have asked me two questions, sir," Leopold replied. "Second question and its preceding implication is patently absurd and possibly offensive. First one is reasonable. Yes, I am surprised. Laws of probability are surely against this kind of thing happening."

"You diplomatic types seem awfully cool about death," Detective Davis said.

"Perhaps. A diplomat dies thousand deaths, Detective," Leopold said. "Every day we must compromise. We watch our dreams of agreement and peace get quashed by compromise and must call it victory. We call lack of courage, imagination and simple mediocrity success and achievement. Physical death is nothing compared to thousand little cuts of compromise. Compromise is death to soul. A good diplomat is already dead. Though I at present feel quite unnerved."

Detective Davis shook his head.

"I swear I must be wearing a kick-me, I'm-an-idiot sign. I haven't heard this much nonsense since graduate school," he said. His voice raised. His face flushed. The former Buddhist monk was clearly close to losing his temper. "You people are too much. You come to my city with your diplomatic immunity and satellite-high view of the human condition—empathy for the idea of man and no clue about caring for the individual directly in front of you. I have a poor little old lady who collected cans and bottles because it made her feel safe with a metal skewer through her chest and a bottle stuck out of her mouth for no good reason, and for once I'd like to hear that one of your kind cared. It would give me some hope for the world."

"I understand exactly how frustrated you must feel, Detective," Leopold said. "I do care, personally, you must understand—but so many do not. Yes, I know you must have your hands full with this lot, and whatever I can help you with I will be most willing."

Leopold's voice dropped into a confidential hush.

"Remember, I did deliver that little bit of information on the gestures yesterday. That must count for something, Detective," the press secretary said. "And I promise to keep my eyes open. But you must excuse me now; I have morning session up at United Nations that I must attend."

Detective Davis gave a defeated shrug.

"That poor woman was our other witness," he muttered.

Leopold delivered a bow and we left Davis in the lobby as we made our way to the street. Once on the sidewalk, we had to cut through a thicket of police officers and a small group of ragged-looking men and women holding burning candles against the bright sunlight of the morning. They were reciting poetry laced with colorful language.

One of the men was carrying a large photo of Abraham Pollop, the dead oral poet. A sign identified the group as the *Friends of Abraham Pollop*. A woman pushed a photocopied sheet into Leopold's hands.

"Don't let his poetry fall on deaf ears," she implored. "Keep the tradition alive."

The press secretary bowed. When we had turned the corner, Leopold crumpled up the piece of paper about the poet without reading it and tossed it onto First Avenue. Five minutes later we were once again headed uptown in a taxi.

Traffic was terrible because of overflow from the Midtown Tunnel, and when we arrived at the United Nations building, Leopold jumped out of the taxi and raced us inside. This time the guards recognized him and waved us through. We were apparently on our way to another conference. Fortunately, I had been fortified by several slices of bacon and a generous dollop of Ms. Ramsey's home fries.

We passed a room with a sign out front that read *Language: Our Common Bond.* The occupants and even the lecturer were in varying stages of a midmorning snooze. Leopold took us down one long corridor, then another, then through a set of fire doors, down a flight of stairs, down another corridor, up another flight of stairs until, finally, we arrived at an enormous kitchen. A sous chef glared at us from behind the long stainless-steel counter where he was chopping thousands of walnuts.

"The dog can't come in here," he said. "Unless he's been skinned."

"Ha," Leopold said. "Talk about diversity."

"It's the United Nations, pal," the sous chef said. "Today I'm stuffing a hundred goats' ears with walnuts. God knows what's on the menu tomorrow."

"I need to speak with Ponce," Leopold said. "It is important. Would you mind getting him?"

He flashed a twenty-dollar bill in the sous chef's direction, but the man waved it off.

"Are you kidding me? Not with this week's anticorruption initiative, I won't," the sous chef said, and disappeared in search of Ponce.

He returned a minute later and resumed his walnut-chopping.

"He'll be with you in a sec," the sous chef said. "He's deep-frying Mars Bars for the Scots."

Soon Ponce appeared, his face covered with

sweat and his apron with flour, egg and chocolate.

"You look terrible," Leopold said.

"It is hell over that deep fryer," Ponce said. "Let's go out onto the loading dock. You don't want Milo Paz to get a look at that dog. He's doing the menu for the Security Council next week and he's promised them yak. But he can't get his hands on it, and apparently dog is *the* yak substitute."

"You can't be serious?" Leopold said. "He can't possibly think that he can get away with cooking dog in this day and age."

"With enough sauce, people will eat anything," Ponce said. "That's my motto. So what's going on? This is very unconventional to meet like this, Leopold."

We had reached the loading dock. Ponce lit a cigarette and flopped down onto a large crate of cabbage. Leopold remained standing, with an almost military uprightness, and I stood beside him.

"You've heard about events of morning at Ms. Ramsey's?" Leopold asked.

Ponce nodded.

"In my thirty-plus years of service, I have never seen such brazen behavior," Leopold said.

"It is like there is goddamn hunt going on. Tell me, Ponce, what is really happening?"

"The stakes are high, Leo," Ponce said. He had a nonchalance that seemed calculated to annoy the older man. It is sometimes considered a weakness of my kind that we can develop feelings of loyalty very quickly. Often the object of this loyalty might seem unworthy (the curmudgeon who rarely showers or the young woman with a princess complex), but we see beyond these failings and look for the best in the individual. We believe when all others have stopped believing, and we—not the doubters and the critics—are typically right. It is the possibility of goodness, kindness and soulful vulnerability that really matters, and we find these things in our masters and drag them out into the light. Leopold might have been an aging spy. He might have done many less-than-reputable things in his life. But at that moment, faced with the insolent Ponce on the loading deck, he seemed like a tired, decent man who thought that something was going wrong and ought to stop.

"Someone higher up is going to intervene," Leopold said. "They always do if things go too far, and I have never seen them go this far. Discreet poisoning, stabbing during a 'robbery attempt'—those kinds of killings were the limit. But sniping in broad daylight and then this grotesque slaughter before breakfast..."

"I'm sure they're *not* going to intervene," Ponce said. "In fact, I'm sure they're the ones calling the shots. There's a rumor going around that the poet and the recyclables lady weren't killed only to frame Imogen. They were killed because they had seen someone else leave that room after Imogen and they were threatening not to stay quiet any longer. Did you know those two old birds were a couple?"

Leopold shook his head.

"Did that silly detective ask after me?" Ponce asked.

"No," Leopold said. "He's sick of all of us. But you're right, I can tell he has his hands tied. But they won't be tied for long if more bodies keep piling up."

"So is that all you wanted to say—that this is outrageous by the standards of the old days?" Ponce asked. "As I said, things are different now. The stakes are higher."

"And still no sense of where girl might be?" Leopold asked.

"One of us knows, but it isn't me," Ponce said. "And if it was me, I wouldn't tell you."

"But sniping was an outside job," Leopold said.

"Sure, one of the guys in the house had support do it," Ponce said. "That's not surprising."

"That's fine," Leopold said. "But what about killing this woman inside house this morning? That could have been any one of you four. It isn't easy to sneak into place. Ms. Ramsey is an insomniac and the halls are seldom empty. There is always someone wandering about. No, I'm quite sure that it was one of you four."

"It wasn't me," Ponce said. "I've been chopping walnuts since six."

"I'm sure nobody knows exactly when she was killed yet," Leopold said.

"Well, I'm on that floor, and the bottle lady wasn't lying there dead when I left for work this morning. And there are witnesses who saw me walk down that hall leaving for work."

Ponce put his cigarette out on the loading dock.

"I don't really get you, Leo," Ponce said. "Why does this matter? You're in town for a conference. Maybe. Maybe not. But whatever it is—you're not at the high-stakes table anymore. This isn't your game, is it? You're an old man now. Things are winding down."

"When you have played game long enough,"

Leo said, "you'll get bit of respect for it and pro-
tocol will matter. Style and proportion will matter. It's dirty game, but there are rules and
dignity. Little people, innocent people being
bounced off to tighten the noose on target is
just not done."

"I've got to get back to work," Ponce said.

"Do you want lozenge?" Leopold asked, offering Ponce a shiny yellow candy from the top
of the roll. "They're ginger and lemon. Excellent
for smoker's throat."

"Sure, thanks."

Ponce took one from the pack and so did
Leo. Then we followed him back inside. When
we reached the kitchen, he looked down at me
and then up at Leopold.

"I'm serious about the dog. He has *main course*
written all over him. Good and fat," Ponce said.
"Milo's a dimwit, but he's determined. He's living at the house too. I'm surprised you haven't
met him. He's from your neck of the woods:
Near *Lower* Pilasia. Oh no, there he is. Hide
the dog."

But it was too late. A smiling man with a
large white chef's hat came around the corner.
He bore more than a passing resemblance to
Leopold—same jowly look and pale skin. My

temporary owner started to back out the door, but I could not move out of his way fast enough. He stumbled over me and leaned heavily into the wall.

"Nice dog," Milo said, sharpening the meat cleaver he was holding, like a cartoon figure. "How much? I'm in market for yak substitute."

"He's not for sale," Ponce explained.

"He's therapy dog," Leopold said.

"Nice dog," Milo said. "Good fat belly. Big brain. Thick tail. I pay one hundred dollars."

Recently I had watched a commercial on television in which an ergonomic office chair was said to fetch $625 and a puppy $100. Although I am an admirer of Milton Friedman, the relative values of the human marketplace can boggle the mind. I doubt if this world will know either peace or be free from lower-back pain until things can be genuinely valued and a dog never fetch less than an ergonomic office chair.

"He's not for sale, Milo," Ponce repeated.

"Ah, but he's perfect," Milo said. "I convince you. You see."

The determined chef put his meat cleaver on the adjacent counter and reached down to give me a pat.

"Friends?" he asked.

He did not reach within three feet. I backed up and delivered an undiplomatic growl.

Milo laughed. "You'll see. Milo convince you," he said, picking up his meat cleaver and disappearing into the walk-in refrigerator a few paces away.

SEVERAL FULL-BODY, head-to-toe shakes were needed to exorcise the prospect of serving as Milo Paz's entrée for the Security Council. Even so, I reflected on Ponce's statement that the dog-focused chef lived in the boardinghouse and, given Leopold's carelessness with locking our door, my mission had suddenly become much more perilous. It is rules and respect for rules that keeps this planet from falling to pieces. A man driven like Milo was a dangerous man indeed. Leopold arrived at the linguistics lecture after the break had fortified the participants with coffee and donuts and part two of five had begun.

And what was my mission exactly? Harry and Imogen were well out of their depth. They were little people, after all, facing international powers. Anyone is little when looking out for one's own interests, one's own happiness, against the interests of some vast government machine. I was more sure than I had been before that Imogen had fled to protect us. She had chosen to become the target, and only a publicized disappearance and rejection of her life could achieve that. Harry had been safe as long as the powers that be thought he had been left. She burned the bridges before anyone else could use them to cross to her treasure (or, at least, this was my belief—and a dog's conviction must count for something). But what could Harry and I do? Where was Imogen? She had fled the young man dead beneath the parachute. She had consumed the same chemical that had rendered him unconscious, but she had somehow not succumbed. My experience with Leopold and the four diplomat/spies (after learning Ponce's job, at least one could be classified as a sous chef/spy) only confirmed what Blinko thought: someone wanted to put pressure on Imogen, but it was certainly an extreme and uncertain way of doing it. One could almost say desperate. And what of my snout stamp from the recyclables lady? Ponce wasn't lying. He hadn't killed the woman. It was not his scent on the victim. That left the other three. If one of these three was guilty, then we would be getting somewhere. I could identify the killer, communicate that fact to Harry and he could pass this information on to Detective Davis, along with other evidence that I could attempt to assemble. Of course, there was the question of the sniper, but Ponce was probably correct on that score as well: it was an assistant of some kind. I did not know how these types operated or how powerful their networks were, but it wasn't too hard to imagine a professional killer lurking in the wings to support one of the boardinghouse operatives. No, the mission was daunting, but it wasn't futile. The murder of the recyclables lady was a tragedy indeed, but it was also a major misstep. If someone could be found guilty of this one killing, then more connections could be made and the chains of suspicion that bound our Imogen would be broken. She would be free (at least from this immediate threat).

The lecturer droned on, drawing no wisdom or insight from the literary masters whom I valued and instead subjecting language to the kind of analysis better suited for diagnosing a knock in a car's transmission or a geriatric's rheumatism. Surely Dante—that great bridge builder—would have something to say about the topic: *Language: Our Common Bond.* James Joyce, whom Virginia Woolf wrongly called a pimply-faced schoolboy, would have obliterated the academic with his potent word music. The poet Auden would have taken an analeptic swig from his hip flask, lit a cigarette and cried eloquent, untechnocratic fire down on humanity's collective head. Yes, my thoughts were darkly inclined, since the better angels of my nature knew the great virtues of linguistic study. Perhaps it was low blood sugar. I *was* feeling a bit *eleven o'clock-ish,* as Pooh Bear might say. As if in answer to my stomach's need, a woman wearing Coke-bottle glasses knocked a crème-filled donut onto the floor right beside me. As Langston Hughes put it: *Sometimes a crumb falls/From the tables of joy . . .*

I downed the delectable in a single satisfying gulp and, thus sated, fell fast asleep.

"REMBRANDT," LEOPOLD'S voice fell toward me like the sound of ashes feathering down a long dark chimney. "Rembrandt, wake up."

A tremendous heaviness was upon me, worse than any of my previous mornings. My paws and every joint ached. My eyelids were sandpaper on the inside.

"Rembrandt," Leopold said. His voice was full of worry and I struggled to move my body. At last I managed to open my left eye. The light streamed in like boiling water, and I shut it promptly. I apologize up front for sounding dramatic, but it is the only way to express the rottenness of Yours Truly's physical condition. Other voices joined Leopold's. Someone poked a toe into my ribs, and I stirred against it by pawing the air. Then I heard Leopold's sharp rebuke.

"Don't do that," Leopold said. "Can you not see he's unwell?"

My brain struggled to reconstitute itself and begin to function. I was on the floor of the lecture hall. I had fallen asleep. I had eaten something before I fell asleep. A donut. A crème-filled donut. A chocolate-glazed donut. Chocolate? How could I have been so stupid? My kind is not supposed to eat chocolate for some reason—a missing digestive enzyme or some such. And now I was useless to anyone and perhaps dying of chocolate poisoning. My appetite had finally been my death sentence.

I slipped back into a painful, semiconscious darkness. From far away I heard Leopold make a phone call. Sometime later I smelled a welcome scent and a familiar voice. It was Harry.

"I'm here, boy," Harry said, and gave me a belly rub. My owner's arrival lifted my spirits, and I managed to raise myself up and look at him. I could scent that he was worried and felt guilty—no doubt for dallying on the visit to the veterinarian. Though it is not my usual way, I gave him an encouraging lick on his shoulder. Then I saw that Haddy McClay stood behind him, which tempered my spirits.

"Is he gonna die, Uncle Harry?" Haddy said.

"I doubt it," Harry said. "He's a tank."

My owner bent down and took me firmly in his arms. With a grunt he lifted me up and carried me out of the room. At least there was one bright spot: I did not have to stay for the rest of the lecture.

Leopold followed us out.

"I'm so sorry," he said. "There is veterinarian on premises. He takes care of secretary general's dogs. I have already called ahead and they are expecting you. We can use motorized cart if you like. I will contact guard."

"How far is it?" Harry asked.

"A hundred yards or so."

"I'll be fine," Harry said. Though I noticed that his breathing had become labored and he strained a bit to keep me aloft.

"When you're all better, buddy, you and I are going to start running in the park," Harry said.

I was not worried. He had made these threats before.

The veterinarian's offices were small and clean. There was a great deal of bleach and ammonia but little richness or diversity of smell. In fact, they were so clean that I could not detect the scent of a single animal. Typically, the veterinary office is a heady place that sends the most levelheaded animal into either euphoria or a fit of nerves, mostly nerves. The smells of hundreds of animals layered upon one another drives the dachshund's blood pressure to dangerous heights and the great bull mastiff into territorial red alert—after all, the dog's most powerful sense is telling them that somehow these invisible dogs are still present (hiding, perhaps, just behind the water cooler or under the end table with the magazines and the pet-insurance forms). But no such reaction could happen in this sanitized place.

Harry was about to put me down on the floor, but a young man in a white medical jacket appeared. He motioned all of us through another door into an even smaller room with a large metal table.

"You can put him here," said the vet, who introduced himself as Calvin Smiley. Harry did as Dr. Smiley directed, and his dog received the shock of freezing metal on his belly.

"Not feeling too great, huh, pup," Dr. Smiley said. Doctors diagnosing humans can usually rely on their patient's ability to express some important facts about the condition. Of course, a vet does not have this advantage, and so Dr. Smiley poked and prodded, kneaded my pliable flesh, plucked at my tongue, dug into my ears and, in a particularly strenuous trial, pulled on each of my four legs.

"He ate chocolate," Leopold said. "A lady told me her donut fell on floor and he gobbled it up before she could stop him."

Dr. Smiley fixed Leopold in a stern gaze.

"Where were you?"

"Asleep," the press secretary said.

"How much chocolate?" Dr. Smiley asked.

"A bit of glaze on a donut."

"I wouldn't worry about it."

"I was told he might have hypothyroidism," Harry interjected, just before it seemed Dr. Smiley might begin another round of leg pulling.

"You've been told he might have hypothyroidism," Dr. Smiley repeated. "Interesting. Has he been sluggish lately?"

"Yes," Harry said. "Very sluggish. It's not that he's the most active dog."

"I can see that," Dr. Smiley said. "You're working on your Buddha belly, aren't ya, boy?"

"He doesn't like to run," Harry explained.

"Not the first lazy Lab," Dr. Smiley said. "I need blood. Lots of it."

A needle was brought out. A very long needle. I could endure the leg pulling and the misguided insult about my work ethic, but, unfortunately, the needle proved my limit. I suffer from *trypanophobia,* or fear of needles, and at the mere sight of that three-inch sharp I once again fainted.

This was merciful because, when I awakened, I saw that the good doctor had several vials of my burgundy in his hand and the needle had been stowed away.

"Very good patient," Dr. Smiley said, apparently unaware that I had lapsed into unconsciousness.

"So what do we do now?" Harry asked.

"I'd like to keep him here overnight," Dr. Smiley said. "We have modest kenneling facilities. He will be able to rest and we will be able to monitor him. In the morning we'll have the results of the blood test, and my sense is that it will probably be hypothyroidism, which is easily treated with regular tablets of thyroxine. But we will know more then."

I tried to catch Harry's eye. If only he could be made to understand that his dog was not to be left in a building that housed a dog-cooking chef. Feeling a bit stronger, I lifted myself unsteadily into a standing position.

"Whoa, boy," Dr. Smiley said. "Take it easy. We have a nice bed all ready for you."

My options were few. I whined, but Harry just rubbed me under the chin and looked resolved to leave me. I was regaining my senses and noticed that my owner wore old jeans and a black T-shirt—his work clothes—and these were covered in dust, paint and drying concrete. His work on the mosaic, I reasoned, must already be well under way. At least he would be across the street for most of the day. Leopold, though, seemed reluctant to leave me. Like most people who suffer from anxiety, he could not help his fear from occasionally getting the best of him.

"Perhaps it would be better, Doctor, if Rembrandt came home with me," Leopold said. "I will be very vigilant. Yes, I think he will do very well indeed in my care."

Harry looked puzzled at my new name but said nothing.

"I couldn't advise it," Dr. Smiley said. "I don't think this is serious, but it's better for him to stay put. He is obviously very weak."

At the doctor's confirmation of my symptoms, I felt a new wave of fatigue break over me, and as if on cue I slumped onto the table despite my best intentions, where I lay utterly unable to move.

"See," Dr. Smiley said. His point resoundingly delivered by Yours Truly. "I can meet both of you here tomorrow morning. I have the owner's phone number? Yes?"

Harry nodded. Apparently he had filled out the paperwork while my trypanophobia had kept me senseless.

I could sense that this outcome did not please Leopold, but he stayed silent.

"Uncle Harry, are they going to put him down?" Haddy McClay asked. "That's what they did with Garbanzo, our cat, when Garbanzo's liver stopped working. They put her down. They said it wasn't serious and then she was dead. Are they going to put him down too? If they are, can we stay and watch? That's what we did with Garbanzo—we watched, and it was really sad but educational too. Mom is always telling Dad to put her down if she ever gets like her mom when she gets old."

Harry shook his head and gave me a gratifying ear rub. I thought I could detect a glistening at the corner of each of his eyes. It did me good to see this.

"And don't you worry," Dr. Smiley said as the trio exited. "There's no more dog-friendly place than the United Nations. He'll sleep like a baby."

When they were gone, Dr. Smiley summoned a large man named Bruce to carry me into a cage in another room. Bruce wore a dark blue jumpsuit and smelled of sardines and cigarettes. I expected to be manhandled but was not. The bottom of the cage was smooth, hard and as cold as the table in the examination room. Bruce noticed this and found a thick blanket to cushion the interior. A water bowl was placed in the corner but no food provided (I couldn't have eaten anyway). I had lost all track of time. I seemed to exist in a timeless place, a limbo with no consequences, and had only the faintest sense that there was a goal or change of circumstances in the works. All of this was because of the fatigue that had exhausted every part of my being. How strange that so much of our experience is dependent on how our bodies feel. I drowsed on and off throughout what I believed was the afternoon. No one visited me, and the fluorescent light in the ceiling panel, with its incessant hum, burned into my eyes even with the lids closed. At some point, Dr. Smiley poked his head into the room, saw that I was still breathing and extinguished the light. I was grateful for the rest this gave my eyes—before realizing that it meant he was leaving for the day. The outer door to the office shut and I was left all alone.

This was very unpleasant. It was more than unpleasant, because, since awakening, I had become more conscious of my situation. I was lonely and frightened and quite sad. I wished very much that I was at home in our apartment, with whatever familiar scents were left after Harry's recent cleanup and settled in among my books and the unfinished canvases of my corner. I write in a way that would suggest that I am "all grown up" and "quite independent." But, really, I am not. Writing is the craft of the illusionist. A writer frames and reframes reality, and soon this mirror trick becomes the world. Language makes me old, but I am only five and a half. At this point canine middle age might be fast approaching, but I'm still saddled with many of the longings of a chronological youth not much past infancy. Home matters, perhaps more than it should. I scratched into the blanket and burrowed my nose in its folds.

Then the outer door opened and the light went on. The good doctor had returned. True to his name, he flashed an extravagant smile. He opened my cage, gave my head a rub and dropped a piece of clothing next to me.

"There's a good boy," Dr. Smiley said. "This'll make you feel more at home. Your owner dropped it off."

It was one of Harry's T-shirts. Most comforting.

I RECENTLY CAME ACROSS a newspaper article that surprised me. The writer maintained that study after study has shown that many humans are afraid of big black dogs. I confess to being afraid of many types of dogs (particularly those trigger-happy nerve baskets that have lashed out at Yours Truly like steroidal cobras in the past), but I find big black dogs amiable. I go by the eyes, which is where a dog's character is to be found. But how many humans go by the eyes? Eyes are a subtle quality. Soulful eyes can be missed by the crude or callous. Intelligent eyes, unremarked. Pleading eyes go unnoticed. We hope to communicate something of ourselves through our eyes, but the world is blind to the projections we cast upon these two-way screens. I have mentioned my difficulty before, but it is worth mentioning again to convey just what it is like to be kept prisoner in a small cage in a dark room in a giant building shared by at least one person who would fancy you for a main ingredient. To be conscious in a dog's body is the equivalent of being constrained in a full body cast with only the eyes showing. I have no facial muscles and my body has a limited range. An owner who is fond of you can make this reality bearable, even pleasant. But a dog on his own is a different matter. A dog on his own is like a desert island far beyond the shipping lanes. A dog on his own cannot pick up a phone and call for emergency assistance.

Harry's T-shirt had been enough to permit me to doze, but sometime in the night I awoke with a start. The outer door had opened and someone was crossing the lobby. The examination-room door opened and the footsteps drew closer. Then the door to my room opened. Milo Paz flicked the light and the fluorescent bulb crackled and hummed to life. The chef was dressed in street clothes and wore a baseball cap. The cap and a broad grin made him look like a child about to do something morally questionable but fun. I edged back into the cage, but Milo had his eyes fixed on me. I had recovered some of my strength, but I doubted whether I could stand and, even if I could, whether I would be able to walk more than a few feet. Running was not possible. He put a hand on my cage and began fumbling with the lock. There was a handle on a spring that had to be depressed at the same moment a latch had to be lifted. Milo had just figured this out when there was a rattling of the outer door. Then a key slipped into the lock and the outer door opened.

"Hello," a voice called out. "Dr. Smiley, are you here?"

Milo stopped fiddling with my cage and flattened himself behind the open door. Footsteps approached. I heard the whine and static of a walkie-talkie, and then a tall security guard, going soft in the middle and bald on top, stepped into the room. He glanced to his right and left. He looked at me, and I, with my lack of facial musculature and vocal cords, could communicate nothing. I decided to bark, and for the first time since the misdirected emotion of my puppyhood I let loose with a raucous volley.

"Shut up," the guard said. "I ain't feeding you."

Then he flicked off the lights and left the veterinary office. His key turned in the dead-bolt lock of the outer door with a decisive sound. *Clunk.* Milo emerged. He flicked the light on, and, as if he had figured out how to open my cage while standing in the dark for those few seconds, he came over to my cage and opened the door with ease.

"Milo is good friend," the chef said. "You see. I convince."

He muttered on like this in a mixture of English and a language unfamiliar to me. Then he donned plastic gloves that had an over-whelming latex smell, which prevented me from detecting any scent beneath them, hefted me into the air and dropped me into a rolling laundry hamper that he had wheeled into the examination room. I was too unwell to resist and lay on my back in a mound of dishrags with my paws in the air. He rolled the hamper out of the veterinary offices and down one long hall and then another. We rode one elevator. And then another. We descended a ramp and ascended a ramp. We rounded a sharp corner, and the hamper listed but did not flip over. And then we were in a kitchen. Not the kitchen that Leopold and I had visited earlier. The smells were not the same, and neither was the ceiling and décor passing by above me. The décor seemed older and dilapidated and there were different spices in the air and the smell of mineral oil from kitchen machinery being worked heavily. I thought I heard several meat slicers operating around me with enthusiastic whirrings of their blades. Thomas Stearns Eliot crowbarred into Yours Truly's consciousness: *I should have been a pair of ragged claws/Scuttling across the floors of silent seas.* Or, at the very least, I shouldn't have eaten chocolate or been a Labrador retriever.

The hamper came to a stop beside one of the slicers. Instead of lifting me out, Milo dumped the hamper like a trash bucket onto the floor, and I rolled to a stop flat on my back among the dish towels. My panic-numbed mind and fatigue-numbed body came to strange, incoherent conclusions. The mad chef would have to skin me first before feeding me to the slicer. No, he would opt to put an apple in my mouth and stick me in the roasting oven hair and all. There are always shortcuts in the kitchen and, like easy-cook lasagna in which one does not boil the noodles first but softens them in the baking process, Milo might simply trust that 450 degrees Fahrenheit would burn off my hair and save him the trouble of skinning. Of course, there would be a lot of smoke and the smell would be awful. In moments of great stress, my mind is prone to take a holiday, stepping away from the hideous probabilities and looking at them with a critical distance that ignores that I am the one about to be scooped into the roasting pan. I also turn to literature. I think of the great scribblers. Their art and, in fact, their lives are like a hedge against the utter senselessness of death. But tonight only Eliot's line ran through my head, alternating with a suffocating sense of this dog's limitations and a craving for home, Harry and Imogen.

A radio in the background played Sinatra. The signal went in and out and the singer's legendary phrasing sounded strained as he worked his way through that tribute to the metastatic ego: "My Way." I have always been most fond of his work in *Guys and Dolls* and, now delirious, wondered if "Luck Be a Lady" would be the backdrop to my demise and whether I would be offered a cigarette, like the condemned in an old black-and-white movie about the French Foreign Legion. But, of course, those who become poultry and pork loins are afforded no such option at their exit, so why should a Labrador? Was I a white meat? Would I taste like chicken or yak? The night, the city, seemed so far away. The threat of one's own death destroys the romantic dream, and each nook and corner of civility, each small joy and peaceful habit becomes a mockery buried beneath the sudden details of biological terror—the details of an extinction that suddenly seems so intimate and so inevitable. Milo had chosen the easy-cook option. He returned with the largest roasting pan I have ever seen. Soon I was being garnished, Sinatra was off and the radio had gone into a commercial for Tempur-Pedic brand mattresses.

I had closed my eyes tight and was looking for some corner of escape deep within myself when suddenly Milo stopped. He dropped his knife. Raw onions burned my nose and I could not smell the chef's emotions, so I opened my eyes again. To my great surprise he was staring at Blinko, who stood in the doorway.

"A dog's not for eatin', mate," Blinko said. Nothing in the massive Australian's voice hinted at it being the least unusual that a Labrador was occupying a roasting pan, which was now ringed with garlic cloves, onions and bell peppers.

His great breadth filled the doorway and loomed, even though his voice had nothing of the looming or threatening quality in it. His was a fresh, clear voice simply making a statement that was not to be questioned, second-guessed or objected to in any way. Milo stood up and wiped his hands on his apron.

"For photographs. My hobby is photography," Milo said. "Dog as food. Food as dog. A meditation."

"That's a pearler, mate. So where's the camera?" Blinko said. "You were going to cook the beast and I've caught you like a barramundi."

Milo nodded.

"We had no yak," he confessed, and backed away from me. "Sorry."

"That's stealing too," Blinko said. "But I'll let you go on that count. You must be a crazy bastard trying a stunt like this. Put the dog back in the hamper and we'll leave it at that. Your next dish is vegetarian."

Milo did as Blinko told him. I was heaved up again and dropped into the hamper. An armful of dishcloths followed and then the hamper was pushed in Blinko's direction. Nothing else was said, and I cannot report with accuracy what gestures and expressions occurred outside my limited vista in the hamper since once again my four legs were awkwardly positioned and my neck was twisted in such a way that I could see little above me.

Soon the hamper was moving and we retraced the path to the veterinary offices. Blinko did something to the outer door when we arrived and we slipped inside. The giant Australian seemed to have little sensitivity to the concept of trespass and a preternatural ability to move around presumably restricted places. I was grateful for it.

When I was back in my cage, Blinko spoke to me.

"You're a special dog, Randolph," he said. "*I* know you're special and *you* know you're special. You might not think anyone knows how special you are, but you need to know that I do. Don't forget it. You keep your eyes open, mate. You keep involved. There's a light at the end of this tunnel, and when you get there, things will be clearer than they are now. I'll do my part, but like I told your owner, I've got to stay at a distance. Tonight was a one-off. I had a sense that you'd be in trouble. I could feel it in me guts. You can't count on me always being around to save the day. You have to get better at looking out for yourself. Things are dangerous and you're in the middle of it. Being dependent is no good. Being sick is no excuse."

And thus having delivered words that left me with the impression that Blinko could see through walls, he gave me a vigorous head rub, rose to his feet and walked out the door, leaving me with one last consolation.

"You'll be apples, mate."

ONE DOG IS CURED

ANOTHER MOST DEFINITELY IS NOT

I SPENT THE REST OF THE night confident that my ordeal with Milo would not be repeated and instead focused on Blinko's strange words. Humans can speak to my kind in many different ways. The most common is the patronizing tone that they also employ against five-year-olds or telephone representatives on the other end of a customer-service line. This tone is characterized by an emphasis on the last syllable and a lilt toward a higher register that turns every statement into a question. As in *Go for a walk*. The question is completed by a word—usually made silly and embarrassing—that suggests that the dog will understand only a childish version of the actual word. In the case of *walk*, this word is *walkie*. Another common tone used by humans is the strange *You-Are-a-Fellow-Sentient-Creature-Even-Though-I-Know-You're-Not-Really-and-I'm-Oddly-Aware-that-I'm-Talking-to-Myself.*

This is employed by both the busy and the businesslike, who cope with the potential embarrassment of a dog's less respectable behaviors by pretending as if they were delivering orders and reasons to a subordinate. As in *Puffins, eating shoes is not acceptable. When we reach the park I will let you off your leash. Let's wait here for the light to change and then we will cross. I can't be late for the meeting, Puffins.* Needless to say, Puffins would soon be a traffic fatality if a leash were not used (I have said that I am unusual among dogs for the cogency of my thought).

But Blinko spoke to me as if he knew I understood. He had called me *special.* My ego was flattered less by this one word than by the fact that it seemed the man wouldn't have been surprised if I had spoken back. What could this mean? It was possible that I was unfamiliar with Australians and thus culturally at a disadvantage. Perhaps all antipodeans spoke to their animals with this kind of respect (though I doubted it, having once read an article about how Australians regularly slaughter their kangaroos even though the animal is featured on their currency—the equivalent of the American going on a hunt for the bald eagle). No, clearly there was more. Blinko seemed to be instructing me but also expecting something out of me.

It was this last part that baffled me the most. Why would anyone expect anything out of me? To outside eyes I was a faithful and amiable dog. I could be counted on to be regular where habits counted. I did not tear up the furniture because of separation anxiety or do unspeakable things to people's legs. But worthy of responsibility? Suddenly the mystery of the young man beneath the parachute, the wealth in the Outback, Imogen's flight, the subsequent murders in the boardinghouse, the Great Game of nations were joined by Blinko's odd assertion and belief. And suddenly, somehow, I began to sense that a thread—only now barely discernible—ran between all of these things, connecting them, and if the right thinking was done and the right facts were learned, that thread would draw them all tightly into one.

"Hound, behold your cure," Dr. Smiley stood outside my cage and boomed. His command wrenched me from a sleep that could neither cure the acid trauma of the previous night's brush with death by roasting nor answer the questions raised by Blinko's strange words. Dreams of Yours Truly being fed like so much pastrami into a gleaming slicer were replaced by image of the good doctor holding my test results in one hand and a bowl of food in another.

Into this bowl he dropped a hot-pink pill and mixed.

He opened my cage and pushed the bowl under my nose. I ate with gusto, and only after I had swallowed the last of the food—dry, tasteless and undoubtedly healthy nuggets—did I note a certain bitter residue lingering at the back of the mouth. This, I assumed, must be the medication that would bring the cure.

"Excellent patient," Dr. Smiley said. "Your humans will be along in a few hours. You'll be standing by then. Drink some water."

I did as instructed.

"It's great when things go easy. You're definitely one of the good ones. I actually feel like I could love animals again," he said.

Then, as if the universe wanted to emphasize that ease was the exception, not the rule, and that loving animals might entail saintly resolve for Dr. Smiley, there was a commotion outside. The vet disappeared through the door and I could hear several people talking at once. Dr. Smiley moved the crowd into the examination room adjacent to my area and I heard everything very clearly.

"Whatever you do, don't call the secretary general yet," one man said.

"What can you do?" a second man demanded

of Dr. Smiley. "There's got to be something that you can do."

"Puppet is dead," Dr. Smiley said. "I've been trying to prepare the secretary general for this day."

"What do you mean, *this day*?" another man said. "For God's sake, you can't die from a hernia."

"It wasn't a hernia that we operated on," Dr. Smiley said. "It was cancer. The secretary general didn't seem to grasp this for some reason. Maybe he didn't want to know. I guess he's a complicated man."

"SG loves his dogs," the second man said. The second man spoke with a kind of authority that the other man didn't possess. "This couldn't be happening at a worse time. SG is brokering a border agreement. It's huge. Front-page news. Make the UN cutting edge again and not some Burt Bacharach, asbestos-ceilinged laughing-stock filled with long-lunching public servants. But the parties are at each others' throats, and, well, you know, SG, Doc, he loves Puppet more than his own kid. He's an emotional man. He *feels* everything. This will be too much for him. He'll be stymied. He'll be flattened. He'll mope for months. Is there any way we can keep the dog alive—at least for the next few days during the negotiations? If we don't, it's gonna be a train wreck."

Dr. Smiley sounded worried that his message wasn't reaching the secretary general's advisers.

"I'm sorry," he said. "But Puppet is dead."

"There's no shot to get him back on his feet? Steroids? Adrenaline?" the man in charge said. "Just for a few days. Then he can die."

"How often does the secretary general see Puppet when he is busy?" Dr. Smiley asked.

"Not much. Maybe at night if he doesn't have an official dinner."

"Did he just say the dog is dead? I'm not getting this," one of the other men said. He was apparently sending messages via his cell phone and had misunderstood the plight of the dog on the examination table.

"Yes, dead. Quite dead. Dead for several hours, in fact," Dr. Smiley said for the third time. "How much contact does the secretary general have with his dogs at times like this? I mean, does he play with them? Does he bring them to the park?"

"No, we do that."

"We can keep Puppet here, then, and tell the secretary general later."

"Impossible. He needs to pet them each once before he goes to bed or he can't fall asleep."

"Once?"

"Once."

"Does he look at them?"

"No," the man in charge said. "He's always reading. Do you know how many briefs, resolutions, memoranda and meeting points the press office produces every day?"

"I can only imagine."

"Reams of paper. None of it matters or actually accomplishes anything—I sometimes think that the United Nations only retains its authority by remaining irrelevant—but SG is very studious, and it's easier for him to read a document than to talk to a human being."

"Allow me to outline the facts," Dr. Smiley said. "The secretary general's dog is dead. You cannot allow him to learn about this until certain negotiations are complete. He has little contact with his dogs but needs to pet them at least once a day before bedtime. He does not look up from his reading material to do so."

"Right."

"Well, then, gentlemen, I think I have your solution," Dr. Smiley said, as if he were about to outline the plans for the next Great Train Robbery.

"Terrific. What is it?"

"Use a surrogate dog, a stand-in," Dr. Smiley

said. "I was going to suggest a taxidermist, but no one does it in twenty-four hours. Besides, Puppet is a common-enough-looking dog. Large and black. Labradoodle. He should be easy to replace—at least for our purposes. In fact, I think, I have the perfect candidate."

"You do?" The man in charge sounded nearly ecstatic.

"I do. He's the therapy dog for the press secretary from somewhere called Near Upper Pilasia."

"Not those backwater savages," the first man said. "They eat stuffed goats' ears."

"This guy seems alright—overrefined, if anything—and his dog is terrific. Actually, his dog is on loan, I think. Look, the owners are getting here in an hour or so. I'll talk to them. I don't see why they'd object. I bet someone from Near Upper Pilasia would welcome the chance to do a favor for the secretary general."

"But what if SG finds out?" the man in charge said.

"He's a professional, isn't he?" Dr. Smiley asked.

"Sure. Except for the crying jags and the manic temper, he's as steady as they come."

"Then he'll understand that you did it for the common good."

"Terrific," the man in charge said.

Clearly both man and beast were dispensable pawns in the great contest of nations. Puppet was removed to cold storage without a single tear, and the man in charge of the SG's entourage poked his head into the room to assess me.

"He'll do," the man pronounced, and consulted a clipboard he was carrying. "We need him at ten tonight when SG has snacktime in the study of his auxiliary apartment on the thirtieth floor."

An hour later, as predicted by the good doctor, I was feeling much stronger. The heaviness of so many days was lifting and I began to realize that at least part of my recent melancholy was the result of this problem in my blood. The idea that a shortage of thyroxine could give me such bleak, Lincolnian thoughts would have been saddening in itself if I wasn't feeling so much better. But sometimes the body buoys the brain, and if sprinting was the kind of thing I liked to do, my legs would be ready to oblige.

I felt so good that I began to pace about my cage. It was this picture of health that Harry and Leopold discovered a short time later. Haddy McClay, after a trial period as artist's helper, had been deposited in the United

Nations nursery. If it was anything like their dog
run, Haddy would likely end in tears.

"There's a good boy," Harry said when I
jumped up and put my front paws on his stomach, something that I had never done before.

Dr. Smiley instructed them on my medication regime and then introduced the possibility
that I serve the ends of world peace by keeping
the secretary general in ignorance about the fate
of his pet.

Leopold reacted strangely to this request.
The press secretary from Near Upper Pilasia began to reek of fear and look visibly nervous. His
right hand even began to shake.

"I'm afraid that I will not be able to accom-
pany Rembrandt on humanitarian mission. My
conference is hosting smorgasbord at the Pierre
tonight," Leopold said. "And, indeed, it would
be unseemly for me to be involved in deception
of any kind, particularly at such high levels."

Leopold was not being honest himself. He
reeked of deception.

"I'll bring him," Harry said. "I'll be in the
neighborhood. Is that okay with you, Leopold?"

The press secretary was reluctant.

"I can't be without Rembrandt for long, you
know," he said. "My nerves have been particularly bad with the mishaps of late. Yesterday and

last night were very difficult without him. The replacement wasn't the same. I have never seen a dog move so little, and he destroyed the curtains with his incessant climbing. Ms. Ramsey was not pleased."

"I'm sorry about that," Harry said. "It was very last minute. I promise you'll have him back for good soon."

A compromise was arranged. Leopold would keep me for the rest of the day while Harry worked across the street at WAHA on his mosaic. Then Harry would pick me up and retrieve Haddy McClay from day care.

I spent the day in another series of lectures on language, wondering how Leopold could possibly have mistaken Jackson's curtain-climbing Guatemalan tree sloth, Marlin, for a dog.

THE EVENTS OF THE PRE-vious week and the discombobu-lation of leaving home only to be shuttled from boardinghouse to kennel had made me forget Ivan Manners's Lorikeet Rescue Fund annual dinner. Tonight was the event, and Harry was scheduled to attend in for-mal dress and as the date of Zest Kilpatrick. The local-television news reporter, perky and brash in the extreme, had asked my owner in a weak moment. While I knew that Harry had not recovered from the blow of learning that his love had shared such close quarters with the op-posite sex, I doubted whether he was ready to "move on." Of course, my owner is a gentleman and would never think of backing out. His table manners may be Stanley Kowalski's, but he is a Mr. Knightly when he doesn't have Chinese takeout in his hands.

Harry picked me up from Leopold later that

afternoon. The press secretary surrendered me at the Dag Hammarskjöld World Pet Unity Area, where we watched two dog walkers deliver sharp blows to each other with pooper-scoopers after a disputed Number 2 went uncollected. A police cruiser arrived to cart them both away.

"Animals," Leopold remarked.

Soon Harry, Haddy and I were aboard the Vespa and speeding crosstown. When we reached the Plaza, Harry turned into Central Park and we whipped up and around the Loop north. Even a few days had made a difference in the foliage, and most of the trees showed signs of new life. And the idea of going home—even if it was only for a few hours—lifted my spirits.

"Whee," Haddy McClay screamed into the wind. I seconded the motion.

When we arrived home, a parcel awaited us. It had been left in the foyer for any New Yorker to steal, like all of our packages.

"What's this?" Harry wondered as we climbed the stairs and he tore open the cardboard box.

"I didn't order Dante and Joyce. I don't need a tote bag with Virginia Woolf's face on it."

I had forgotten my impulse purchase. Fortunately, Harry had too much on his mind to pursue the matter, and the parcel was thrown down next to the bookcase, where I would be able to explore the books and tote bag in a free moment. Harry searched through the closets for a tuxedo he believed he had once owned, until he remembered that Imogen had donated it to Goodwill. This left him with either his business suit or Grandfather Oswald's polka-band outfit (Grandfather Oswald was a talented accordionist, who had toured Michigan and Illinois on weekends after his service in the war). If this was the movie version of our story, Harry would have been forced to choose the polka-band outfit, which would have offered a funny shot or two of my owner speeding through the streets of New York on his Vespa, looking ridiculous, and then arriving at the black-tie affair looking even more ridiculous. Thankfully, no matter how strained it seems at times, this is reality, Harry is not insane or beyond embarrassment, and he chose the business suit.

Unfortunately, reality also dictated that young Haddy McClay must practice her violin per Iberia's instructions. For a half hour, Harry's niece scraped away on her instrument, inflicting grievous harm to my sensitive Lab eardrums. Then Harry said it was time to go. Apparently all of us were invited to Ivan Manners's Lorikeet Rescue Fund annual dinner.

The phone rang. It was Zest Kilpatrick. I suspected that she was not pleased to learn that she would have to find her own way to the dinner and we would meet her there.

"I'm sorry, Zest," Harry explained. "There's just no room on the Vespa with Randolph and my niece. I'm thinking of installing a sidecar."

But when we arrived, Zest stood on the curb looking utterly composed and, by human standards, stunning. Her television good looks had been amplified by strategic use of makeup. A facial made her skin shine and countless hours at the gym ensured that she was both muscularly sound and aglow with aerobic health. To underscore the "aha" effect, she wore a profoundly red gown that hung from her shoulder like a celebrity in search of the paparazzi. If a certain critical shrillness has entered my description, I apologize. I was merely thrown on the defensive by Zest Kilpatrick's pincer movement on my owner's vulnerable male front.

I needn't have been. Harry was more interested in fixing the kickstand on the Vespa, which was sticking in its housing.

"Hi, Zest. I'll be there in a minute," Harry

said, reaching for a wrench in the Vespa's tool kit.

While Harry attended to our vehicle, Zest occupied herself speaking on her cell phone about a breaking news story that she apparently now wished she was covering.

"Get the widow to say what you need, Caroline. You can do it. You didn't get hired in a number-one market for nothing," Zest said. "Tell her that you totally understand what she's going through. You know, the usual. Lay it on her. Get her to talk about their vacations. Their kids. Their first kiss. Whatever. And if that doesn't work, do the public-needs-to-know stuff. That usually works. People think they have to be noble when someone croaks. Don't get me wrong. The story's decent television without the widow, but decent isn't good enough for Channel Eight."

"Are you ready?" Harry asked, having fixed the kick-stand and gathered his charges in respectable order for entrance into the dinner.

"I'm sorry for that. I guess I can't help talking shop," Zest said, her voice sliding down the register from hard-edged newswoman to soft, fuzzy and approachable.

"That's okay," Harry said. "I've been wanting to fix that kick-stand since I got this thing."

Many of the attendees of the Lorikeet Rescue

Fund annual dinner had brought their birds and were making their way up the magnificent marble staircase that rises from the entrance hall of New York City's Discovery Society. Bird and man ascended beneath crystal chandeliers that evoked great nets and alongside tapestries showing famous discoverers past. These discoverers included Teddy Roosevelt emerging from behind a palm, holding a dead armadillo, and Sir Isaac Newton stirring a cauldron.

"I don't think this is going to be your average black tie," Zest said. "And by the way, I notice my date isn't, strictly speaking, black tie. More business formal."

Harry smiled.

"It was this or my grandfather Oswald's polka outfit."

"Wise choice," Zest said.

Due to my owner's chronic lateness, we had missed the reception and the stuffed mushrooms and baked brie (though I managed to Hoover a good number of wayward appetizers off the carpet). My appetizer maneuver reminded Harry that it was time for my medication, and another hot-pink pill was thrust between my jaws. Not even the strong quince paste in the baked brie could diminish the bitterness of the medicine. I searched for water

but there was none in sight. Zest seemed to notice my dilemma but charged ahead to the as-
signed table.

"This is us," Zest said. A small flag declaring
the table Channel 8's rose from the center.
Although there were eight places, only two were
occupied by a couple who gave Zest a wave and
then began to fork their salads as if they were
loading silos.

"We paid ten thousand bucks for this table.
Our CEO is a bird freak but he couldn't make
it," Zest whispered to Harry and gestured at the
two. "Be nice to them. They do makeup. They're
geniuses, but if they hate you they can make you
look like death."

They took their seats, and I sat on the floor
between Harry and Zest and assumed a watch-
ful posture. Harry supplied Haddy McClay with
some paper and crayons and she began to draw.

"You're a good daddy," Zest said, a sudden
maternal appetite opening like a deep New York
pothole between them. Zest blushed. "I meant
uncle. Uncle. Uncle. Uncle. I'm an idiot."

I could see how her vulnerable persona could
be disarming and even appealing, if one was not
aware of the steely character that lay beneath it.
Fortunately, Harry seemed only too aware.

A waiter arrived and we learned that there

was a choice of Dover sole or filet mignon. I wondered what would happen to the three meals that had been destined for the unoccupied places at our table. With the treatment of my thyroid deficiency, my appetite was even more robust than usual.

Harry ordered filet mignon for himself, a special order of fish fingers for Haddy, but nothing for his dog. After the waiters had taken all the orders, Ivan Manners gave a speech that seemed to equate the plight of rainbow lorikeets with the deficiencies of the American educational system and the nuclear arms race. Then he pointed to the band and invited everyone to dance.

"Thank you," Ivan said. "Remember, a bird without seed is a bird in need."

"Want to dance?" Zest asked Harry. Harry was digging into his salad as if the emergency exit to the evening might be found there.

My owner nodded, said that he'd like to and then escorted Zest onto the dance floor, where they danced through two fast songs (during which Yours Truly's ears suffered high-decibel torture), one slow song and another fast. At first Harry looked awkward, but during the slow song he seemed to relax, and when they returned to their seats (Zest making quite a show of being out of breath as if she were on a soap opera), I detected a distinct change between them. Harry was warmer and more open than I would have expected. That strange telescoping effect that happens between two humans in romantic situations was suggested in the way that Harry turned his chair toward hers and Zest turned her head, supported on her palm, toward his head. I had been present when he and Imogen began dating and, being a much-interested observer, noted many of the details of human courtship: the conspiratorial quality that enters the voice, the lingering eye contact, and the moment of self-revelation followed by a short explosive laugh. It all said the same thing to me: how the distance between very different people is bridged by the mysterious processes of the blood. Harry and Imogen were very different people indeed, but their physical attraction was matched not by a specific affinity of tastes—they were quite far apart—but by an affinity of spirit. But human attraction is such that physical attraction can mask the kind of differences that should doom a relationship from the start. I was prejudiced in Zest's case, but I could not imagine that the woman capable of squeezing a story out of a widow for the evening news had the kind of sensibility that could match Harry's more compassionate and artistic depths. But dinner passed with familiarity growing between them. They shared each other's main courses, and when dessert arrived, Harry split his crème brûlée (Imogen's favorite) with the television reporter, who admitted that she was watching her weight but "absolutely loved" crème brûlée.

"It's been hard . . . this past year or so," Harry offered after the dessert was gone and they had returned from a second slow dance to a table from which the insular makeup artists had fled and beneath which Haddy McClay had curled up to sleep. Yours Truly remained between the couple, despite several attempts by Zest (when Harry wasn't looking) to be bribed away from his station by food held beneath the table on her far side. The candles burned down into their holders.

"It's been hard since she left," Harry said.

"You mean your girlfriend?" Zest said.

"Girlfriend," Harry said, testing the word. "*Girlfriend* sounds so casual. I never think of her that way. We would have been engaged the next day."

"One of my best friends has been engaged five times," Zest said. "It happens. Trial and error. Mainly error, I guess. I'm sorry, that was a stupid thing to say. I am always saying the wrong thing."

"No, I'm sorry," Harry said. "I don't know how we started talking about this."

"Because it matters to you. And if something matters to you, I'm interested," Zest said, perhaps on the wings of one red wine too many. She edged her chair closer to my owner and tried to push my substantial flank out of the way with her heel but was unsuccessful.

"Look, Harry, I really, really like you. I'm not usually this forward, but I think you're great. I'm not a psycho, I'm just someone who has always seen what I want and gone for it."

I could sense Harry weakening. The loneliness and doubt of so many months without confirmation of Imogen's side of things had accumulated into a heavy load that was crushing him. He had been a guard at the shrine to their memory until the shrine was shown to be a sham. He had lived for more than a year alone. Without enough solitude a man loses himself, but too much solitude makes him vulnerable— even when he denies it—to another's touch and some outside confirmation that the universe isn't just a reflection of his limited self. Solitude provides perspective, only to strip you of it, if you indulge solitude too much. As one wag has put it: if you stare into the abyss long enough, it starts staring back. I could not stand between these two forever. A physically attractive, charismatic media personality had targeted my owner. Powerful forces of attraction were at work. I should have made a greater effort to communicate with Harry what I knew about Imogen while I had the chance. What had I been doing? Ordering books on a stolen credit-card number, snuffling food scraps off the floors of New York and getting sick and almost eaten?

"I've got a confession to make," Zest said with a choreographed flip of the hair and an intense use of her left eye. "I noticed you when you were on TV and they were interviewing you about your girlfriend. I thought you were adorable, so adorable. And then when I saw you at that dog spa..."

Harry leaned in toward Zest. I thought of averting my eyes. I thought of intervening. I could give Zest a kiss on the lips like some proactive cartoon dog taking one for his master, but something other than my pride and the thought of Zest's lipsticked petri dish held me back. This was Harry's moment, and he would have to decide its outcome on his own.

Zest fluttered her eyes and she repeated herself.

"I just really, really like you."

"Zest, you're a lovely girl. But I would be lying if I said that this can go anywhere. It can't. I can't. Maybe I'm like that widow for you. Someone who's attractive because they're showing they can be hurt. I'm not that goddamn widow."

"Harry, that's not it at all. I'm coming on too strong. Let's just stop. I'm all work, and when it comes to this kind of stuff, I never know what to say. I guess I just think that you probably need closure."

My owner put his head in his hands. At first I thought Harry might cry, but instead he steadied himself.

"I'm not that widow."

"I know," Zest said.

"No, you don't know," Harry said. "Seeing you tonight has changed things for me. It's made things clear. I was slipping. Now I'm not. You're very attractive. You're successful."

"Whatever that means," Zest said.

"You are successful by any usual measure," Harry insisted. "And you're not the kind of woman that a man would walk away from. But I can't forget Imogen. And even if I could forget her, I don't want to. And it doesn't matter where she is. Or who she's with. It doesn't matter if I'm an idiot to think this way, because it's my choice. And it wouldn't matter if she was here and told me to forget her. Because I wouldn't. I wouldn't forget her smell or the way she says certain words or is nervous in crowds or breathes when she's asleep or holds a pen or a photograph or a book. I've made up my mind. I know what I believe, and it doesn't matter what she believes or what she doesn't believe. I knew her at her best, and that's the person I know she is. And I believe that there's no such thing as closure, because if I don't see her again, and hold her again and get one more chance to spend a Sunday afternoon doing absolutely nothing with her again . . . I've said enough, Zest. I'm sorry."

Harry woke Haddy up, and with one cranky child and a saddened television news reporter in tow, we left the the Discovery Society, descending the grand staircase in silence beneath the ever jolly Roosevelt with his dead armadillo. At the curb, my owner hailed a cab for Zest, and in cinematic fashion she turned to him as she slid into the backseat.

"Good-bye, Harry," Zest said. "I only wish someone says those things about me someday. Too bad it couldn't be you. Imogen is a lucky woman. I hope she knows it."

IN GRAPPLING WITH THE important truth of his love for Imogen and sparing Yours Truly a disturbing scene in which my vision of a happy family was wounded by the amorous Zest Kilpatrick, Harry had forgotten what time it was. As Zest's taxi disappeared into the night and my owner began to rev the Vespa, it occurred to him to ask the Discovery Society's doorman the hour. Neither Harry nor Imogen ever wore watches.

The answer was sobering.

"Ten-thirty," Harry shouted. "We're late."

We squealed off toward the United Nations, treating all manner of street signs and traffic indicators as mere suggestions rather than law. Ten minutes later my owner had parked the Vespa outside the tower's entrance, removed the license plate and hustled all of us through security.

"I'm bored," Haddy McClay said. "*And* I'm tired *and* I don't think you're being a very good role model."

"You'll survive, chestnut," Harry said.

The elevator creaked skyward, and when it stopped at the appointed floor several minutes later, we were met by the man in charge from Dr. Smiley's office.

"Lucky—you caught the fast one. People have gone mad in Shaft Three."

He was an unlikely-looking aide to a high-level diplomat. He had a boxer's forearms and giant, rock-breaking hands that looked a bit ridiculous holding a glass of milk and a plate of chocolate-covered marshmallows.

"You're just in time," he said.

"I thought we were late."

"Technically, but nothing runs on time at the United Nations. I'm just bringing SG his bed-time snack now. If you can wait in that room for the next ten minutes, then everything will be just fine."

The aide pointed at a large conference room walled off by glass from the corridor. It was filled with people who were screaming at one another.

"Are you sure?" Harry asked.

"Oh, you mean them," the aide said. "They've

been in there so long, I'd almost forgotten about them. They're not SG's problem, but he lets them use the conference room. They've been haggling over water rights for a decade. Every so often the negotiators rotate out. This is the fresh crew. They're very animated, but after a week of this they tire. There's coffee in the corner and juice in the fridge. I'll be back in a moment."

We slipped into the room and sat as far from the arguing horde as we could. Haddy McClay resumed her nap. Harry drank a cup of coffee and then turned the Styrofoam cup into a miniature sculpture with a plastic spoon. I watched the dozen or so men and women clustered over a map. At some point, the entire group departed the room. I took the opportunity to examine the matter over which they were arguing. I was already familiar with the dispute, since it had been covered in a feature article in *The New York Times* some months earlier.

As the aide to the secretary general had suggested, these two nations had wrangled over this issue for nearly a decade, and the dispute had produced more than a few fistfights as well as several marriages. The dispute was not really about water at all but about drilling and fishing in a river that ran between the two countries. One of the more colorful aspects of the article (and the reason I think the *Times* ran the story in the first place) was the map itself. As the wrangling had progressed, the map became littered with small plastic pieces that represented various aspects of the dispute. There were tiny drilling platforms and fishing boats peppered all about an enlarged map of the river. These pieces had been in movement over the years as the terms of future propositions were presented and, inevitably, rejected by the delegates. Although I frequently find journalists to be sloppy with their facts (too eager, perhaps, to escape the wrath of a deadline-focused editor and not concerned enough with the eternal posterity of truth), as I hovered over the map I found the writer to be quite accurate in his description. The little pieces were there jostling for position: red for one country, green for the other. There were even deep tracks in the map where a piece had been moved back and forth several times along the same path. The whole idea of these negotiations struck me as ridiculous, because neither country had ever had very much luck feeding its citizens and yet here their pampered delegates were, arguing themselves hysterical over game pieces that in most cases represented only theoretical rights. The stress of recent days had accumulated to dangerous levels within me, and now, looking down on this absurd game board that represented millions of lives, I felt like that god/giant that Voltaire described in one of his more subversive writings on the human condition. I had read the passage only once before Imogen plucked it away and returned it to the library, but I vividly remember the concept of a giant coming to earth and making a mockery of various human conventions of church, state and tradition. He was a massive, universal figure. The kind of creature whose very existence makes man look very small indeed and reminds him of how large and indifferent is the cosmos that surrounds him. The giant could gulp down Lake Geneva or straighten Italy's boot.

Harry's head was in his hands. Haddy McClay was snoring. The delegates were nowhere about. I began to move their pieces around with my snout. I was that giant fiddling with absurd human conventions. To one side, I gave all the drilling platforms. To the other, all the fisheries. Let there be commerce between them. Let them trade each for each. A simple solution heedless of the true marketplace perhaps, but a solution nonetheless for these technocrats who could come up with no solution while their people went hungry. If there were Alpha-Bits present, I would have laid out more-complex instructions or perhaps drafted an entire treaty. But this would have to do. I suspected that my tinkering would only cause more arguments and accusations of dirty tricks in the matter of the little plastic pieces, but Yours Truly could not be bothered. I had taken a mental holiday—the whole exercise was a bit like the roll with the liverwurst.

I had just hopped down when the aide to the secretary general returned.

"He's ready for the dog," he said. "I'll take him. You two can stay here. It'll only be five minutes."

The aide led me down the hallway and into the anteroom of what looked to be a private apartment. There we met Flowers, the deceased Puppet's companion. Puppet's death had only served to make the already paranoid Flowers even more acutely so. *Paranoid,* the word that had been used by Leopold to describe the secretary general's dog, was not strictly speaking correct. Flowers was a hypochondriacal compulsive, a nerve basket in grave fear of doing anything not habitual. The condition was so serious that Flowers ignored me completely, not even attempting the customary glandular hindquarter sniff or the off-to-the-side non-threatening glance. I was grateful for the absence of the hindquarter sniff but offended by Flowers's utter disregard of my presence. After observing her for a moment, I realized that this wasn't rudeness but that she, like so many with her condition, was trapped within a mental prison of fear. For every two steps forward, Flowers would scratch the floor three times, as if not to do so would cause her sudden death. If she turned her head to the right, then the next move would have to be a sharp turn to the left. She seemed spastic, and all of her movements, except her tail, were strictly controlled.

"Flowers, you stay here," the aide said as he pulled me past the other dog and we passed down another short corridor. "You've already gone in."

The walls of the corridor were white and lined with photographs of the secretary general meeting various people, including the pope and someone dressed as a Hershey bar. The career diplomat wore the same practiced smile in each picture: a sensitively designed expression of empathy that could be interpreted as either pain or joy.

The aide pushed open the door to the library.

The man himself sat at the other end of the long, book-lined room in a plush green chair that swiveled with a squeak because it was old or needed oil.

"Mr. Secretary," the aide said. "Here's Puppet."

The secretary general looked up and delivered his practiced smile to no one in particular. There was an enormous stack of documents on his lap and another one on the floor beside his chair. An empty glass and plate sat beside the stack of papers, and at the corner of the secretary general's mouth were two dark smudges from the chocolate marshmallows.

"You can leave the dog," the secretary general said. "And go home. It's late."

"But Mr. Secretary," the aide said. His voice was measured, but he reeked of nervousness. Clearly SG was going against habit.

"You shouldn't be too surprised, Bertie. They're my dogs, after all. Though you wouldn't know it because I never see them."

"Would you like Flowers?" the aide asked.

"Definitely not," the secretary general said. "Things are tough enough without me needing to be reminded of my nerves. Just watching that dog makes me worried. Check her out, by the way."

"I'll bring her to Dr. Smiley in the morning," Bertie said. "Perhaps I should bring both of them then, sir. I don't mind waiting tonight. It will be easier in the morning."

But the secretary general returned to his papers and did not answer, and Bertie was left to unhook my leash and hope for the best.

I decided that the soundest approach would be to get as close to the secretary general as possible so that he would be least likely to recognize that I was not Puppet. Bertie left the room, and without warning the secretary general launched into a monologue.

"Puppet," the secretary general sighed. "I am tired of this life. You know this. How many times have I shared my secrets with you?"

Apparently, Puppet served as confidant to the secretary general. I wondered what burdens the loyal black dog had borne for his master that led to an early grave. Cancer is a funny thing. I have sometimes wondered if it is a rebellion of the body against the excesses of the soul.

The secretary general did not wait for any gesture on my part to acknowledge just how many secrets had been shared with his dog but launched into a sweeping statement on his day and its challenges. He complained that the shock absorbers on his official car needed to be replaced.

He fretted that he had eaten too many beans at lunch and would "pay for it" the next day. He spoke ill of the Brazilian representative for a minor indiscretion but praised the Austrian emissary for his taste in clothes. The secretary general was a complex man whose scent is best compared to a ripe cheese. It was not a bad smell. It was not a good smell. He was neither sharp nor mild, but there were layers of sophistication tempered by time and experience. The experience had made him interesting, but he had paid a price to get to a place few men ever reached. Yes, he was a complex cheese just on the cusp of spoilage. His monologue confirmed it. He stretched out his long corduroy-clad legs and smoothed his forehead with his palm.

"Puppet, things are getting worse. The world had stabilized there for a while with the two superpowers, but we're past all that now. It's a brave new world that looks a lot like it did before the First World War. Alliances faltering. Competition for resources. But there are differences that make the moral picture even more troubling. Overconsumption and starvation. Millions of rich and billions of poor. A modern self-absorption that makes concerted social action unlikely. We've always been a sounding board at the United Nations, but now it seems that nobody is listening. A war is coming, I'm certain of it. But that's not what bothers me anymore, Puppet. I'm starting to think about all the victims of our compromises ... of my compromises.

"Today I remembered something that I had forgotten for so many years. It happened when I was a young man. I had just passed the civil-service exam and was stationed in Cuba—the Cuba of Batista. His regime was reaching its end. Castro's forces were squeezing its legitimacy on all sides. I was representing my government at the dedication of a school in the countryside. A demonstration was organized by middle-class women protesting the policies of the Batista government. The army was called and began to use billy clubs on the crowd. Women fell. There was blood and screams. Even though I had no authority, I demanded that they stop attacking the protesters. They did. But when I returned to the embassy, my superior was furious with me. He told me that it was undiplomatic. He told me that in the future—if there was going to be a future for me as a diplomat—I was to turn my back. That is what a diplomat did."

The secretary general sighed and scratched his ear. I thought his story sounded vaguely similar to something I had read by Graham Greene.

"I've been turning my back ever since, Puppet."

He shuffled his papers.

"And now I am being asked to turn my back again. Or, more accurately, not turn toward something against which I have kept my back turned for too long. The United Nations has always tried to stay above the dirty games that nations and corporations play. We say that we maintain our credibility by taking the so-called high road. But we have been used and now it has gone too far. Diplomacy and the games of nations are big games. We measure human lives in percentages and probabilities. Cost and benefits are not about individuals but about a portion of the population pie. Fifty thousand live or die because seat belts have been required by law or not or because war has been declared or not. We never think that little man living in that little village will never see his wife again because we spent another month dawdling over lunches and cocktail parties and not resolving the dispute that will cost his life. If we thought that, I suppose, we could never see enough of the big picture to get anything done. We smile for the photographers and shake hands and things happen in the dark of night and the women scream and the children disappear or they don't.

But somehow all of this stays abstract, because we're drunk on the big picture. If we can reach such-and-such number or a certain projection, then those things that happen to those individuals might not happen."

The secretary general sighed again.

"Puppet, I can't turn away anymore. The credibility of the United Nations—whatever credibility we still have—is at stake. The nations and the corporations have been practicing their dirty games all along and I've known about it. We all have. But now they are so much more blatant and so much more destructive. I know that the knives are out because of what they are willing to do in our backyard. This uranium situation, for example, and this innocent girl."

I had been mulling over the secretary general's hard-earned observations on statecraft, but mention of uranium and an innocent girl made me snap to attention. What did the secretary general know? Was this what Ponce meant when he spoke of those at the highest levels being aware of what had gone on at the boarding-house?

"This has never happened before, Puppet. One murder. Then a second. Then a third. Three murders. Unprecedented. And all three certainly connected in some way to our institution. There has always been cloak-and-dagger work and agents at the UN, but this is so brazen. All the authority of the United Nations is being called upon to protect the guilty and chase down the innocent. I am sick of it. I am being called upon to put our credibility and decency in the balance by quashing this investigation. Yes, I'm being asked to keep my back turned while one of the big players makes off with one of the little people's rightful fortune. I'm sick to death of myself, because up until tonight I wouldn't have thought twice of letting this happen. But something's changed. We need to have a housecleaning. We need to throw the dirty parties out. We need to stop this. Of course, everyone denies knowledge of who did the killings. Honor among thieves. They're all afraid that if they stop playing by the winner-takes-all rule and start behaving honestly, their pasts will catch up with them. And they're right, of course."

The secretary general sighed again.

"What am I supposed to do, Puppet? The United Nations will suffer if I act, but if I allow it to serve as cover for this kind of outrageous criminality and intrigue it will suffer even more. Perhaps this time I won't turn my back. Then again, perhaps I will."

The secretary general seemed to have exhausted himself. He fell silent and returned to his stack of documents. A few minutes later Bertie appeared at the library door.

"Are you still here?" the secretary general asked.

"If I could take the dog, sir."

The secretary general nodded.

"I'm done," he said.

Bertie escorted me from the room. He met Harry in the conference room, where the feuding delegates had once again assembled over their maps. The debate seemed more heated than before and I suspected they had discovered my intervention. But we left before I could learn more.

"Same time tomorrow night?" Bertie asked Harry at the elevator.

"I don't think it's a problem," my owner said. "The other guy will be bringing him."

Leopold surprised us by picking me up downstairs at UN headquarters. He seemed more nervous than usual.

"It has been a difficult night without Rembrandt," Leopold said. "I am very shaky."

I did not want to leave Harry, but the secretary general's admission had emboldened me. There was more to learn at Ms. Ramsey's boardinghouse.

THE LOBBY OF THE BOARD-inghouse was quiet when Leopold and I arrived. A lamp burned in the corner and the plug-in fireplace was aglow. Leopold had begun to lead me up the stairs when someone behind us cleared his throat. The press secretary snapped his head around and seemed about to jump into the air. But then he saw it was Ponce.

"Oh, it's you," Leopold said. "What do you want?"

"We need to talk," Ponce said.

"Not now. I am exhausted."

Leopold turned to go.

"Yes, now," Ponce insisted. "Or I will tell the Near Upper Pilasian government who you really work for."

Leopold's scent suddenly changed from a defiant nervousness to a genuine fear. But neither his voice nor his body betrayed this change.

"Ponce, you're a jackass. A young idiot. At best this is stuff of pulpy espionage movie—creeping up on me like this with your accusations. What does it matter who I work for?"

"It would matter to the Near Upper Pilasians, since you are traveling under your country's diplomatic protection but working for a foreign government and doing things that will be destructive to us all."

"What do you know?"

"More than a few things."

"Name one."

"You are involved just like the rest of us in the uranium matter."

"That's ridiculous. I just arrived."

"Perhaps. Although our people believe you have been in the United States longer than you say. But that isn't the point. You are a handler. We're not sure who you're handling, but you are part of this mess, and now the secretary general himself is considering getting involved and cleaning house."

"The secretary general," Leopold said. "That is extraordinary. But really, Ponce, this is stupid. Even if I was involved, what would it matter? There are a number of players in this house."

"It would matter because your operative has made serious blunders that have jeopardized us all. Someone has to be held responsible or all of us will be."

"Have you spoken to anyone else about this?"

"Only my side," Ponce said.

"Not Otis Cheng, Max de Tocqueville or Lindmar Wingman?"

"Of course not," Ponce said. "Any one of them might be your operative."

"So this crusade to clean house is crusade of one man—you—and one country?" Leopold asked. "Or perhaps it isn't even one country at all. Perhaps it is only matter of one man looking for little something extra. You are wise to be interested in real estate. It will be good to have such things set aside for your retirement. So you would like me to pay you something to stay silent?"

Ponce nodded.

"Very well," Leopold said. "I will see what can be done."

We began to climb the stairs.

"I need to know in twenty-four hours. No less than a million euros."

"It isn't ideal, but I will make arrangements," Leopold said.

When we reached our room, Leopold made a phone call.

"You must stop," he said into the phone.

"This is well beyond what I signed on for. This is simply not the way things are done. Enough is enough. People are aware of my involvement. The secretary general is going to be taking action. Hello? Do not hang up on me. Hello?"

Leopold redialed the number but no one answered. He was worried now. Very worried. But this did not stop him from changing into his pajamas and brushing his teeth. Perhaps, when one lives the stressful life of the diplomat/spy, one becomes equipped to handle even crises without disturbing routine. In a very short while, Leopold was settling into bed beneath Imogen's stars, aglow and as indecipherable as ever.

"Rembrandt, go to sleep, for God's sake," Leopold said. I must have been pacing. I curled up and for a short while I managed to fall into a light sleep. Sometime after midnight, though, I was awoken by the sound of voices down the corridor. It was Max de Tocqueville, Otis Cheng and Lindmar Wingman. They seemed to have paused on the landing and were discussing something in hushed tones that would have been out of the reach of all but my dog's ears.

"He obviously did it," Cheng said.

"I'm sure you're right," de Tocqueville said. "But he could not have done the first one."

"That's right," Wingman said. "Then it was one of us."

"Us or Ponce," Cheng said. "But who are we kidding? None of our governments would endorse such lunacy."

"The stakes are high," de Tocqueville said. "Things are not the same. The game has gotten very dirty. I heard that the secretary general is considering intervening."

"There's no question that someone is going to have to be sacrificed before all this is done," Wingman said.

"But the girl will get away from all of us," Cheng objected.

"She'll resurface and we'll all have another chance. But this cannot go any further," de Tocqueville said. "Or all of us will be finished here. And I, for one, love New York."

"So what do we do? And how can I really be sure that neither of you bumped off the last one?" Lindmar Wingman said. They continued to climb the stairs and their voices dropped out of range.

Blinko had been confident that there were four diplomat/spies involved. Leopold made five. But Leopold had been speaking to someone on the phone whom I presumed was neither Ponce, de Tocqueville, Cheng or Wingman.

And these last three were speaking about someone as well. They could have been speaking
about Leopold. *He could not have done the first one,*
de Tocqueville had said. But certainly none of
the three could suspect that Leopold was behind the killing of the poet at tea. There was a
sixth figure then.

Leopold continued to snore. I needed to
learn more. At the very least, I needed to get a
snout stamp from each of them. Fortunately,
per usual, Leopold had neglected to lock the
door. Although numerous movie dogs drive au-
tomobiles, pick locks, and the like, Yours Truly
is not paw-capable. I have never attempted to
twist a doorknob, knowing only too well how
unresponsive my rigid limbs and floppy paws
are. However, this door was different. Instead of
a knob, Ms. Ramsey had opted for the homier
and snout-friendly latch lever. In a moment, I
was out in the hallway and proceeding with
haste toward the men.

They had just arrived at the next floor when I
reached them.

"Hi, doggy," Lindmar Wingman said, and
reached down for a pat. One sniff and I knew
that Wingman was not the recyclables lady's
killer. Otis Cheng was equally friendly and

equally not the killer. Only de Tocqueville remained, but he threatened to disappear.

"Good night. I trust we're on the same page," de Tocqueville said as he opened his door. But not before I was able to deliver a solid snout stamp to his right calf and get a good sample.

"Get away," de Tocqueville snarled. "Now I'll have to wash these."

De Tocqueville, though terminally snobbish and Labrador-hostile, had not killed the recyclables lady either. The three men disappeared into their rooms and I was left standing in the empty hallway. There was no doubt now. I could not be certain who had killed the young man under the parachute or the oral poet, but I did know that neither Leopold, Ponce or these three had killed the recyclables lady. The killer was someone else.

I had begun to saunter back to our room when another door opened and things became decidedly worse.

MILO STOOD BEHIND ME. This was unwelcome. Particularly since he still wore his chef's apron. "Friends with Milo now?" asked the zealous chef with exotic tastes as he knelt down beside me. But I was already moving toward the stairs. Unfortunately, despite being on the heavy side, Milo was remarkably quick. He put me in a headlock. I struggled. I tried to bark, but he was pressing very hard on my throat and I could make no sound. Then he pulled me into his room and closed the door. He held me in place with one arm, and with the other he began searching for something on his desk. The lamp caught something shiny: the point of a needle. My trypanophobia was drowned out by terror of Milo and his culinary designs. I needed to stay conscious. I needed to fight. But he was so much stronger, and a moment later I felt a sharp pain in my hindquarter as the needle punctured the skin and its contents were injected into my body. The mystery was over for me now. The search for Imogen done. Harry would face the loss of another creature he loved and I would join the ranks of "the disappeared." The light seemed to brighten, then fade. There was a trickling sound in my ears. But as my eyes became unfocused and I slipped into darkness, I gained one last concrete revelation through my nose: Milo had killed the recyclables lady. He was the sixth man. Then all went black.

"Rembrandt, you lazy dog."

Once again, Leopold's voice fell down toward me like ash down a high chimney. He was somewhere far above me.

"A lazy and fat dog," he continued. "There are countries where lying around like that would get you a one-way ticket to the dinner table."

I felt a nudge in my ribs (I still had ribs) and sun—late-afternoon sun—stung my eyes. This was good news. Tremendous news. My spirit wanted to race around the room and knock over all the furniture. I was alive. My body was less responsive.

"Come on, Rembrandt," Leopold said. "It is time to get up now. You have been asleep all day. Here, Ms. Ramsey has prepared you special dish, and I have added your medicine."

A large bowl of food was placed beneath my snout. I was lying sprawled across the floor of our room and apparently had been lying there for some time. I managed to open my eyes and saw that, indeed, it was late afternoon. The sun was already bathing the façade of the building opposite in golden yellow light.

"Eat, eat," Leopold said. "Your incapacity has left me incapacitated, my friend. I have barely ventured out all day. I missed several lectures because of you, but we won't tell the ministry, will we?"

Whatever drug Milo had pumped into my system wore off quickly, and I ate the food Leopold presented with gusto. I assumed it must be the next day. Leopold sat at his desk, typing on his laptop.

"Remember, I must drop you at secretary general's tonight," Leopold said. I lay on my back and stared straight up. The message of the ceiling still eluded me. I began to search for letters and assemble words from the letters I could find. I realized I must still be groggy when I formed the sentence: *I AM IMOGEN.* But the sound of Leopold's fingers on the laptop keyboard soon drove this less urgent puzzle from my mind. After all, I knew that Milo had killed the recyclables lady. I also had reason to believe that Milo had been the poet's shooter. And if Milo had killed both witnesses to the first murder, then he had probably killed the young man under the parachute as well.

I needed to relay this information to Harry and through Harry to Detective Davis. Certainly if the police arrested Milo, they would find evidence that would connect him to the crime. And if the secretary general was no longer going to tolerate international espionage in his house, nothing would stand in the way of prosecuting the guilty and clearing my innocent mistress. Perhaps this was too simplistic, but it was a start.

Leopold looked at his watch, muttered and hurried off to shower down the hall. Fortunately, he kept his computer open and online. I climbed up onto the chair and got to work. This time I moved faster through the virtual environment (I bypassed several book offers, including a strange one that combined the collected works of Kafka with the memoir of a celebrity chef). I composed a message to Harry that read:

> Investigate Milo, resident at Ms. Ramsey's boardinghouse and cook at United Nations. He is responsible for recent killings. Pass on to Detective Davis.
>
> —Holmes

I used the name Holmes to remind Harry of the spirit detective who had guided him through our last misadventure with strategic use of Alpha-Bits cereal.

Just as I pressed SEND, I became aware of a weight around my neck. The screen briefly turned black and I saw my reflection. My therapy-dog ribbon was now attached to a new collar. A collar is never completely comfortable, but this collar was quite heavy and it was uniformly thick, a bit like a black garden hose with a leash clip at my nape. Who had placed this new collar on, and why? I shook and noticed that the underside of the collar seemed to have small protrusions that scraped against my skin, and one segment was slightly warm, as if it was generating heat. Then there was a smell. It was quite distinct and familiar, but at first I couldn't place it. I heard Leopold coming down the hall. What was that smell? Somehow this was important, I thought. Somehow this was something I needed to convey to Harry.

Leopold stopped in the hallway. He had dropped something. I heard him strain to pick it up. He fumbled it. He strained again. Then I recognized the smell. It was similar to the smell of gunpowder—a gritty, salty smell (I had smelled gunpowder when Harry discharged

Grandfather Oswald's .45). It was an explosive of some kind.

Leopold picked up the object and kept moving. And just as he reached our door, everything came together and I understood. Out of my dark and woozy memory I felt the collar being secured around my neck and heard Milo's accompanying mumbles: *ten o'clock...damned secretary general...the only way...* Milo wanted to use me to blow up the secretary general of the United Nations. As impaired as my memory of the previous night was and as outlandish as this conclusion seemed, I was certain that it was correct. The secretary general was threatening to take action that would likely end in Milo's arrest. Milo was taking the opportunity to frame Leopold, another diplomat/spy (why else would he have passed up the chance to roast Yours Truly?). The two protrusions were part of some kind of triggering device, and tonight, at or about ten p.m., the secretary general and I would be blown to pieces together with his milk, chocolate-covered marshmallows and stacks of documents. I needed to get this second message to Harry, but already the door handle was turning. I closed my e-mail and hopped back down onto the floor.

Quite aware of the heaviness around my neck.

WE REACHED THE UNITED Nations just before eight o'clock. Despite having an acid bath of nervousness and terror sloshing about my belly, I was also quite in need of a Number 1 and 2. My mind was racing. If Harry had chanced to read his e-mail, the authorities might already be racing into action against Milo. But that was unlikely. Even though it was Saturday, he was planning to spend the day at work on his art commission and away from his computer. And as far as he was concerned, I was in Leopold's care for nearly another week. The other night had been an exception because of my medical condition. Now that this condition was stabilized, I was once again on my own.

Fortunately, though Leopold had not seemed to notice my new collar, he did sense that a visit to the Dag Hammarskjöld World Pet Unity Area was in order. We slipped through the gate.

Night had fallen. Only a few dogs wandered about in the dark while their owners huddled in the circles of lamplight near the entrance. Tonight, the standout canine was an exquisitely refined yet spirited dachshund named Dulcie. Dulcie stayed near her owner and from time to time added a welcome English accent to the culture of the dog run.

Leopold sat down on a bench and sucked on a lozenge.

Clearly whatever I was carrying around my neck could not be so sensitive that it would simply explode. There must be some triggering device. And it could not be a timer, since my visit to the secretary general could be delayed again as it had been the night before. No, Milo would need to be near enough to know that I was at the target.

I shuffled among the wood chips on the opposite side of the dog run and delivered my Numbers. Somehow between now and then, I needed to get this collar off my neck. Then I saw him, beckoning to me from across the yard: Mahatma Gandhi. The great Indian statesman stood frozen in advancing stride, his loincloth miraculously held aloft while his two arms were outstretched at waist level in a gesture of welcome and peace. The index finger of his right hand was independent of the rest. It was longer and gleamed in the lamplight because it had been burnished by people rubbing it over the years. It was this index finger that offered Yours Truly the hope of salvation.

I hurried to the base of the statue. Leopold was distracted by an Alsatian, which was standing on the bench and attempting to steal a second lozenge that the press secretary was trying to deposit on his tongue. I jumped at the index finger but missed and fell back down on my paws. Then I jumped again, and this time the finger slid between the collar and my neck, just as I had hoped. For a moment I thought I might accidentally hang myself, but then the collar began to stretch and my neck and head slid backward out of it. I fell back to the ground for a second time, but this time the bomb collar was left dangling from Gandhi's finger.

Leopold had driven off the Alsatian and was ready to leave.

"Come on, boy. I want to be especially early for secretary general," Leopold said, stressing for any interested diplomatic ears the fact of his high-level meeting. When we reached the sidewalk he muttered what I thought must be an expletive in his native tongue.

"Where on earth is your collar?" he asked, but

quickly dealt with the problem by fashioning a temporary collar from a plastic bag he found on the sidewalk and hooking my leash to it.

The guards at the entrance to the General Assembly waved us through. They were no longer interested in determining whether the press secretary's dog was a bomb. Had I not disposed of the device myself, this would have been the wrong night for them to come to this conclusion.

Bertie, the secretary general's aide, met us at the elevator as he had the night before. But this time the conference room Bertie took us to was entirely empty of arguing delegates. Leopold seemed to be aware of the long-running dispute over fisheries and oil rights and asked Bertie where they were.

"Haven't you heard?" Bertie asked. "They've settled their dispute. Some visionary rejiggered the board while no one was looking, and the resulting terrain was pleasing to all involved. The formal settlement will be signed within days. It is a great victory for the United Nations. If you can just wait here, I will bring the secretary general his bedtime snack and then the dog can visit. He did a beautiful job last night. The secretary general was much soothed."

At fifteen minutes to ten, Bertie appeared

and said it was time. He led me down the corridor toward the secretary general's quarters. Several of the conference rooms that lined the hall had people milling about in them, hunched over papers, listening to speakers, and just outside the room closest to the secretary general's quarters, sitting in a comfortable chair, I saw Milo. He was dressed in a tailored suit and equipped with an attaché and a sheaf of documents that he seemed to be poring over with great intensity. Anyone would have mistaken him for a delegate gathering his thoughts and studying his notes before making a case in one of the busy conference rooms, and they would have missed that his right hand was plunged into a pocket, waiting expectantly for the right moment to push a button.

Bertie and I passed in front of Milo, but the aide stood between us and blocked Milo's view of my neck as we entered the secretary general's quarters. Milo did not notice that the collar had been removed.

The secretary general was in no mood for a monologue on the challenges of his work, and Bertie never left us alone. I received a pat on the head and a quick ear rub and was quickly escorted out of the room. The entire exchange took less than a minute. We emerged to find

Milo looking visibly shaken. Bertie led me down the corridor toward Leopold, and Milo followed.

"Thanks," Bertie said. "SG wasn't into him tonight. One more night is all we need and then we'll break it to him about Puppet. Can you do it?"

Leopold nodded and smiled, but his smile vanished when Milo stepped into the room after Bertie bade the press secretary good night.

"What do you think you are doing?" Leopold asked. "Are you mad, you Near Lower Pilasian ass? We can't be seen together like this. That day in the kitchen was bad enough."

Milo shut the door behind him and, as Leopold attempted to stand, shoved the older man back into his seat.

"You sit," Milo said. "And you listen."

Milo was not only imperative in his tone, the Slavic rockiness of his English had disappeared and he spoke like an Oxford don, as did Leopold now.

"This is unacceptable," Leopold said. "I am your handler. Not the other way around. How dare you push me down like that? Your superiors will be hearing about this."

"You killed the young man," Milo said. "And you had me cover your tracks because you knew that it would only be a matter of time before those two old fogies revealed that you had passed them in the hallway before you were ever supposed to arrive. They weren't just witnesses to the girl leaving the room. They were witnesses to you leaving that room earlier in the day. And you could never pay them enough to keep them quiet. All of that was fair enough."

"Just part of the game," Leopold said.

"Part of the game," Milo echoed. "But you were going to sell Near Lower Pilasia out, you Near Upper Pilasian bastard. You were using us."

"Indeed, I still am," Leopold said. "In a short while the police will be arriving to arrest you for the murder of Abraham Pollop and the poor old lady who liked her recyclables. They will also be arresting you for the murder of the young man. And possibly even the attempted murder of the secretary general, which would have implicated me had Rembrandt not been so clever to remove your primitive bomb collar. Of course, had he not done so, I would have. Did you really think I wouldn't have noticed? Why would you try to kill the secretary general? This sort of stuff is madness. You and your people can't take our game to this level. It ruins it for everyone."

Milo looked stunned.

"I don't believe you," he said. "The police

aren't coming. Why would you call them? I would only turn you in. Oh no, we're going to leave here and we will figure out a way to get the girl into our good graces. You will get us our uranium and then both our countries will have a fine bargaining chip to use with the great powers. King Bougainvillea's fifteenth-century vision of harmony between our two lands will finally be realized."

"You're right," Leopold said. "Of course you're right. Why would I call the police?"

Leopold took out his lozenges and put one in his mouth.

"Would you like one?"

Milo nodded. Leopold gave him a lozenge—this one was orange, not yellow, like the others.

Milo put it in his mouth.

"I'd like to be friends," Leopold said. "We have been too long at war, and this recent alliance must not fail."

But his dog knew that the press secretary was lying, and a moment later Milo knew as well. There was a commotion in the hall. Police officers led by Detective Davis charged toward the conference room. Finding the door locked, two of the policemen shattered the glass and stepped through the hole. Their guns were drawn and pointed at Milo. But the man only stared at them. Then, before anyone could react, he fell dead at their feet.

"Are you alright?" Detective Davis asked Leopold.

"It wasn't ideal," Leopold said.

"Gandhi lost half his arm," Detective Davis said. "The man was a maniac."

"He put something in his mouth," Leopold said. "I think he might have poisoned himself."

A HALF HOUR LATER, Harry and I were walking away from the United Nations and toward the Vespa. My owner was taking me home. Leopold had decided quite suddenly that he no longer needed a therapy dog. Milo's revelations prior to his death were disturbing. Leopold, the real murderer of the young man, was free. I would not make a good diplomat, because my concept of right and wrong is not so shaded or ambiguous. This could not stand, but I would need to have access to the computer or some other message medium to get this point across to my owner, and then what...It was hard to imagine how someone like Leopold— whom I now knew was as crafty and wicked as they come—would not somehow escape justice.

Harry took the Velcro license plate out of the pocket of his Driza-Bone rain gear (a light drizzle had begun to fall) and reattached it to our

vehicle. He had just straddled the bike and begun rolling it backward onto the street when I
heard a whistle. My mistress had rejected the
use of silly dog names in favor of a set of distinct
whistles. There was the whistle that meant
"stop." The whistle that meant "come." The
whistle that meant "sit." There was even the
whistle that prompted me to roll over.

Now, beneath the gentle sound of rain and
the distant rush of traffic up First Avenue, I
heard the whistle that meant "come." This time
I saw my mistress before I could smell her. She
was standing some fifty yards away, next to a
taxicab double-parked at the First Avenue entranceway to the FDR. She was dressed in a long
black cloak and her face was concealed under a
hood, but there was no mistake. She whistled
"come" a second time.

And I did.

"Randolph," Harry shouted. But I was running as fast as I could toward my mistress. I
sprinted across the drive and then up onto the
sidewalk opposite and down the hill. Harry was
somewhere far behind me. And then I reached
her. I had imagined this moment so many times,
but the proximity to my mistress overwhelmed
any dream.

"Good boy," Imogen said, and knelt down be-

side me. She put a warm hand to my cheek. Such
a warm hand. And in the sliver of lamplight and
the luminescence of the falling rain, her eyes
flashed and looked with such deep love and
kindness into my own eyes. And her scent. It
was Imogen: authentic and lovely, but so heavy
with desperation and loneliness. She could not
conceive of a way out. That is what her scent
told me, and it made me instantly very sad.

"Now hold this and don't let it go except for
him," she instructed me, and thrust an envelope
into my mouth. Then I noticed that she was
looking up at something behind me, and I realized that Harry was approaching and that my
mistress was fighting the urge to stay. She almost lost, but instead she put her other hand on
my cheek, clasped my head firmly and repeated
her words.

"Good boy."

Then she got into the cab and it sped away.
Harry was indeed approaching, but not on foot.
The Vespa pulled up just as Imogen's taxi turned
onto the FDR heading south. I knew he had
seen her.

"Give me that," Harry said, snatching the letter from my mouth. "Get on."

I jumped onto the back of the Vespa. Harry
snapped up the sides of my box and soon we

were on the FDR, searching for her taxi. The rain battered our faces, and buckets of water sprayed over us from passing cars. Then, just when it seemed that we would never catch her, Harry spotted her taxi. He kept on its tail even though a fog began to develop as we reached the southern tip of Manhattan Island. Then the taxi stopped, and she jumped out and began running toward the Staten Island Ferry. A boat was getting ready to depart and Imogen raced toward the ground-level loading ramp. We abandoned the Vespa and gave chase. As the deckhands began to lower the gates, Imogen weaved among the stragglers and disappeared into the crowd. Harry and I got on board a moment before the ferry jerked free of the dock and began to throb its way out into the channel and the frigid early-spring waters of the harbor.

"What do you think you're doing?" a deckhand cried out at our backs, but we had already run inside and were tracking her down the side of the boat, past drowsing Staten Islanders heading home. Imogen pushed through the far doors onto the forward deck, and a few seconds later we did as well.

The rain was falling heavily now. The fog was thick but was being driven about by a building wind. Only a few dozen feet of the water ahead of the ferry was visible. It roiled like tar, and occasionally the ferry would strike a wave the wrong way and a sheet of foam would spray up onto the deck. And all the while the giant boat throbbed forward on the strength of its massive engines, crashing through the fog and the rain because it had somewhere to get to.

There was no one on the forward deck except for Imogen. She had climbed over the protective rail that separated the passenger deck from the semicircular iron wedge that extended over the water and the frothing bow.

Harry and I raced to join her, but then her eyes met Harry's and we stopped and she took a step back.

"Everything's in the letter," Imogen said. "And everything's also in the stars."

Then, as if she had been practicing the maneuver from infancy, she turned her back toward us, gave herself a short running start and dove off the boat and into the water.

Without any hesitation, Harry jumped the rail and threw himself into the water after her. I followed. Hitting the water was like falling into a mound of hard-packed snow, and despite my ample water-dog coat, the freezing liquid immediately began to suck life from me. Before I even made it to the churning surface, my limbs had grown heavy and seemed almost incapable of keeping me afloat. My head broke into the air but was just as suddenly pushed back under by a heavy wave. When I broke to the surface again, I saw Harry struggling in the water and realized that the back of the ferry had passed us, its lights being dimmed to black by the fog. Then the ferry and the throbbing of its motors were gone and we were left with the driving rain, the fog and the waves. Harry kept shouting out Imogen's name, but there was no response. Water-polo player though he was, I could tell that my owner was losing strength. We were both losing strength. We treaded water for several minutes, and then I knew he was slipping. His head dipped beneath the water for a moment, so I swam under his arm to buoy him up. But he was heavy, and besides the waves and the sound of the rain, everything else was black and silent.

A DOG DRIES OUT

———————

A LETTER EXPLAINS A DEATH

THE CALLER WHO RE-
ported a man and a dog overboard
on the Staten Island Ferry remained
unidentified. But he was prompt. In fact, he was
so prompt that, against the odds, the New York
City Police Department Harbor Rescue Unit
managed to pluck the two out of the water.

They did so just as Harry and I began to sink,
rigid and limb-frozen, into the deep. At first I
thought the helicopter's spotlight was a cold-
induced hallucination, a trick of the eye before
the final curtain. Then someone was beside us
in the water, and Harry was lifted up into the air
to the helicopter that beat heavily just above
the fog. Soon I was being hoisted skyward as
well. I don't remember much of what happened
next. Harry managed to tell them about Imogen
being in the water, but he was in worse shape
than me, and the rescuers worked hard to raise
his core body temperature with warm liquids,

blankets and vigorous rubbing. I was left to shiver my own way back to normalcy on the floor of the helicopter.

The helicopter trolled back and forth over the waters, panning the satin swells with its powerful spot and coordinating the search with two boats below. The diver who had rescued us seemed ready to throw himself back in the water at any sign of life, but there was no sign of life. At one point, he gave me a pat and pinched my generous belly.

"You're a living flotation device, aren't you, buddy," he said. "Without you, your owner would have been a goner."

He smelled strongly of rubber from the gaskets of his dry suit, the sealed outfit that protected him from the frigid waters. It was a powerful smell and familiar, but in my still-diminished state I could not place it.

After twenty minutes, the helicopter turned to home. Harry, who was regaining his strength and his senses, began to get agitated, but the crew told him that the boats were still searching.

"Imogen," Harry moaned. "Imogen."

And then my owner put his head into his hands and cried.

Two hours later we were back at our 90th

Street abode. Harry had improved so much after the cold-water shock that a hospital stay was deemed unnecessary. Detective Davis had met the helicopter at the ER, and after a great deal of debate and gentle coercion had convinced Harry that going to his own home to wait for any news was the best idea. They hadn't rescued anyone else from the water and it was very unlikely that they would. Imogen was gone—at least, gone beyond the reach of the New York Police Department Harbor Rescue Unit.

Detective Davis understood that he needed to focus Harry's mind on the concrete. How had Imogen looked as she jumped? What had Imogen said? What was in the letter? As battered and as pained by the emotional tumult of the evening as my owner was, Detective Davis needed him to focus, and so sitting in our apartment, Harry summoned great reserves of strength and did just that.

Together, detective and artist pored over the letter, or what was left of the letter. There wasn't much. But what had survived changed everything.

> *Harry, I don't know what you know. What you don't know. I'm not my mother. I'm not a murderer. I didn't kill Richard. Maranovsky*

> *did. He drugged him. He drugged me. He thought*

All the rest was ink stains and meaningless fragments, with the exception of this compelling snippet near the end:

> *At the risk of sounding melodramatic—you can find me in the stars.*

Detective Davis began to smile.

The clock on the microwave said that it was three in the morning. The apartment was silent. Haddy McClay was asleep in the bedroom, having been entertained by a babysitter all day and evening while my owner worked on his mosaic. Harry shook his head. "Why are you smiling?"

"This confirms what we already suspected."

"What do you mean?"

"I've been earning my salary, Harry," Detective Davis said. "The young man beneath the parachute had a name."

"Yeah, I know, Richard," Harry said with bitterness.

"Richard Camier," Detective Davis said.

"Imogen's boyfriend."

"Hardly. Richard Camier was the son of Madame Camier. Madame Camier was the nanny who raised Imogen. Richard and Imogen were like brother and sister. Madame Camier lives in France. Or, rather, lived in France. She seems to have disappeared."

"What?"

"We believe Richard was trying to protect Imogen when he was killed."

"And you believe Imogen's letter—that she didn't kill him?"

"We do," Detective Davis said. "You know we found equal amounts of chloral hydrate in both drinks."

"You mean the knockout drug?"

Detective Davis nodded.

"When we found traces in both glasses, things began to make less sense to me. Why would Imogen knock herself out? And if she had planned the killing, why would she have run away, leaving all the evidence? So we hit the streets and the bars of the East Village. There were several descriptions of a woman who matched Imogen, disoriented and lapsing in and out of consciousness. Some good samaritan even called the police, but by the time they arrived she had disappeared."

"But why was Richard wearing a parachute?"

"He was a BASE jumper. In fact, he was quite well known around Europe for jumping from dangerous heights in heart-print boxers. He had bought the parachute that day. I guess he was just trying it all on together."

"So you should grab Leopold."

"Mr. Maranovsky is under surveillance. He's at the boardinghouse tonight and we've got two cops on him," Detective Davis said.

"How did you know before the letter?"

"I didn't," Detective Davis said. "But I never trusted that guy and I made sure my bases were covered. I've just texted my guys to bring him in."

Detective Davis's phone rang.

"I see," he said. His voice was suddenly subdued. "I'll be right there."

Detective Davis hung up the phone.

"What's wrong?" Harry asked.

"The murderer has murdered himself. Leopold Maranovsky just swallowed an orange lozenge and croaked."

A FEW DAYS LATER, HARRY took me to work at WAHA. After hearing about the harbor swim, Iberia had promptly removed Haddy McClay from our midst. Jackson had offered to give Harry a week off without penalty in light of recent traumatic circumstances and the great progress my owner had already made on the mosaic, but Harry was determined to keep working. What he had accomplished in his first week on the job was impressive. A female eye dominated the piece—an enlarged version from the still-unfinished portrait of Imogen in our living-room corner.

We passed through the lobby and into his workshop in the back.

"There will be stars," Harry muttered, stepping over enlarged photos of the stars on the ceiling that he had taped to the floor as a kind of model.

We had copies of the same photographs at home and I had lingered over them for a long time over the last few days, trying to puzzle things out, but to no avail.

Now Harry stopped above these photos. As he stared, a change came over him.

"I know where I've seen these before," he said. "She showed me a photograph of a night sky. It was on Curaçao."

My owner was elated.

"My God, that's where she's going."

Then he was sad again. Detective Davis had already suggested that Imogen might still be alive and on the run, but the improbability of her survival in the water that night baffled them both.

"But how? How could she have gotten out of the water? It almost killed me and I'm a swimmer."

Then his dog filled in the blank with a scent memory. I remembered the strong and distinctive rubber smell of the rescuer's drysuit gasket. I had smelled it beneath all of Imogen's other smells when she stooped to put her hand on my jowl. My mistress had been wearing a drysuit. She had expected us to follow her onto the ferry. She had wanted us (and perhaps others) to see her plunge into the harbor. It is not lack of

swimming skill that kills most cold-water drowning victims, it's hypothermia.

I needed to communicate with Harry and
ready us for the next step. As soon as I was able,
I would e-mail this revelation to my owner.
Perhaps I would even be so bold as to purchase
tickets to the Caribbean and buy appropriate
travel guides and other reading material for the
journey (Graham Greene's *Our Man in Havana*
or Hemingway from his Cuba and Key West
periods). Complimentary tote bags might even
be necessary.

Harry and I would soon be leaving
Manhattan and traveling south.

DON'T MISS

J. F. ENGLERT'S

other charming
Bull Moose Dog Run Mystery,
A DOG ABOUT TOWN

Available from Dell

A DOG
ABOUT TOWN

MEET RANDOLPH.
A DOG LIKE ANY OTHER DOG—
BUT WITH A NOSE FOR MURDER...

J. F. Englert

LYELL OVERTON MINSKOFF-Hardy, literary light and cultural personage, perished a few days before Christmas beneath a stainless steel toilet on the Upper West Side of Manhattan. With his fly open. Harry, my owner, prone to accept all explanations involving the paranormal, believed the death had a supernatural flourish. Almost from the start I thought Harry quite mistaken. Overton's death had nothing to do with ghosts, spirits or the occult and everything to do with science, human nastiness and greed.

I first learned of Overton's death upon the return of my owner to our humble walk-up apartment. I had been rereading Robert Pinsky's excellent translation *The Inferno of Dante*, an artifact from Imogen's time in our lives, when I heard the familiar clump-clump on the stairs and the jangle and click of locks being opened—notably more urgent than usual. I did not have time to close the book or even move too far away from it. I imagined my owner's imminent surprise. The book would be the first thing he would notice, no doubt. The reading light that had been off when he departed would be the second.

I was wrong. Harry was in such a distracted state that he noticed nothing out of the ordinary. Rain dripped from his Driza-Bone jacket and pooled on the kitchen floor. My owner is a broad-shouldered, strapping fellow, standing almost six foot three, and you would never guess that his regular regimen of physical fitness had long been derailed by frequent retreats to the La-Z-Boy recliner with buckets of fried chicken and takeout Chinese.

"A great man is dead tonight, Randolph," he pronounced.

I could think of several great men who were dead that night. Dante Alighieri, Florentine poet, first among them; Sir Winston Churchill, a close second, but I did not so much as growl a qualifier.

"A famous man," Harry emphasized.

He crammed what looked like a Maryland crab cake into our deeply troubled refrigerator, the interior of which had remained a shadowland of petrified broccoli and pizza since the bulb burned out months before.

"Lyell Overton Minskoff-Hardy." Harry spoke the dead man's name with a kind of reverence.

It is a point of pride that I remain well acquainted with the biographies of luminaries past and present. I do this chiefly through newspapers and magazines. There is much truth to be gleaned from the gossip columns. Rich treasures of it. I had already assembled a full mental file of notes on the man Harry named and I drew from it now.

Lyell Overton Minskoff-Hardy was two men really. There was the patrician figure, Lyell Overton, whose name evoked English estates and private libraries where wolfhounds stretch before the sputtering hearth and leather-bound volumes lie open awaiting the return of some tousle-haired savant from Oxford. An appropriate image, I think, for he was tall and graceful in that insouciant, underclassman way—a perennial student and college man, his torso forever sheathed in the invisible, but palpable, entitlement of the varsity letter sweater.

The Minskoff-Hardy contribution was gritty, ethnic and glamorous in a hard-won sort of way. It was Broadway via Ellis Island and the Five Points—vintage New York. Minskoff-Hardy could be urbane and world-wise, but also, as are so many native New Yorkers, hopelessly parochial, predisposed to view with suspicion anything not found or imported to their narrow island. Minskoff-Hardy was brash and full of colic, demanding and impatient. But more than anything, Minskoff-Hardy was ambitious and his ambition had wounded, scarred and made an army of permanent enemies along the way.

Both men inhabiting the hyphenated identity died that night with their flys open, their eyelids slightly ajar and their last bon mot left unspoken.

These matters of temper and temperament are now locked in his dead heart, but his death—and this moment with Harry in our cramped but cozy Upper West Side abode—would bring out that inner being in Yours Truly concerned with the murderous significance of details and the disastrous consequences that stem from small gestures. All such questions of the heart and the character are my concern because the detective is the last true humanist, standing at that lonely intersection where observation and reason meet emotion and intuition revealing the secrets that measure our fragile, inconstant, but extraordinary beings. How ironic, then, that I am not even human.

Yes, that is correct. I am *not* human.

You see, I am a dog—not a scoundrel, a cad, a rascal—no, not a dog in that sense, but an actual dog, *Canis familiaris*. One of the most familiar and lovable (I only repeat the general perception): a Labrador retriever. A Labrador retriever is defined by Merriam-Webster as "any of a breed of compact, strongly built retrievers largely developed in England from stock originating in Newfoundland and having a short dense black, yellow, or chocolate coat...called also *Lab, Labrador.*" Faithful to that definition, I am indeed compact and strongly built (though bulging at the midsection from my owner's generous feedings) and black but for a wisp of premature white on my chin that serves to impart a sort of sage-like impression.

I am also sentient. I can think. I can remember. I can understand that as the teller of this tale I had best get most of this explanatory material over with at the beginning. Like the reader, I compare the past and the present. I strategize and calculate. This is not a possibility entertained by the Merriam-Webster definition. The competent editors of that publication are not to blame for the oversight. Most dogs certainly do not behave in ways that would suggest sentience (though I might also add that most humans do not either as is apparent from the hastiest of glances at the newspapers). Moreover, there is at present no way to penetrate my species' muteness. Science is unable to plumb the depths of our cerebral cortices and discern the life of our minds.

Even so, among my brothers and sisters, I am unique. Where other dogs babble, I sing. Where they follow tangents like they are darting from scent to scent, my thoughts are precision-guided. If you could speak our language, you would understand. It is a challenge to extract a single relevant word from one of my brethren let alone a competent sentence and forget reasonable analysis altogether. It's all myth, rumor and constant distraction with them. What makes my kind endearing to humans makes them difficult for me to endure. It is a mystery why I am different. Genetic mutation, something in the water my mother drank during her pregnancy, my rearing, who knows? I came to consciousness, I suspect, in much the same way a human child does: sticky scraps of reality gradually collaged into a bigger picture within which an identity was assumed.

"Randolph, tonight was unbelievable," Harry said finally. "It's going to be all over the papers tomorrow."

He forced the refrigerator closed with a grunt. I had the momentary sense that something might try to escape.

"One minute Overton was at the table telling stories: a taxi ride with Truman Capote; strip poker with Kerouac; arm wrestling with Fidel Castro..."

Harry reached behind the toaster for his emergency cigarettes. He shook one free from the pack, lit it and put the rest into his pocket.

"Halfway through dinner, Overton gets up, walks down the hall, then there's a sort of yelp. I expected that he would burst out into the dining room with a joke; instead he was dying on the bathroom floor in a pool of urine. A woman found him. I think she owned the apartment. At least, she acted like she did, but I don't think she is the one who invited me."

Harry had been invited to assist at a séance that night. The invitation had come through the mail with no return address. Harry wasn't too sure who had invited him, but he accepted anyway—lately he had become vulnerable to the promises of the paranormal and immersed himself in that otherworldly network of charlatans and misty-eyed believers. It was a fascination that was trying my patience even though I understood the tragedy that had caused it—a tragedy that had crippled me as well and made it impossible to act with any decisiveness for many months.

"She acted like she owned Overton too, because she kept nagging him. When she found him, she screamed. We didn't even get to the real part of the séance. Overton wanted us to contact his first wife. She had died on their wedding night. He said she was his true love..."

Harry's voice trailed off, leaving only the hollow, tinny sound of rainwater down our drainpipe and his crisp inhale. I knew he was thinking of Imogen; talk of true love always had this effect on him. Imogen was *our* tragedy.

Less than a year earlier Imogen had left our apartment for an evening walk. She was going to Zabar's to buy some bread. She often made this trip on the nights she returned home early from her work as an archivist at the Morgan Library—that fabulous New York institution endowed long ago by the solitaire-playing tycoon J. P. Morgan. Imogen liked to buy bread at the end of the day. It was usually marked down, but more than this, the idea of getting bread daily appealed to her romantic nature. She told Harry that it made her feel like we were living in Paris and she had ducked down to the *boulangerie* for a baguette.

But that night she didn't return. Harry launched a massive search. He enlisted the police. He rallied friends. He chased down every lead he received and spent hours in excruciating vigil by the phone. Weeks passed. The police finally found her red beret under a bench in Riverside Park. The assumption was that she had somehow fallen into the water and drowned. At least that was one assumption, but darker visions of my mistress's fate haunted me. Her body was not found and she remained a missing person.

Harry and I had been living a sort of half-life of false starts and impossible expectations ever since in the same apartment to which we three had all moved so happily, filled with future promise. Harry and Imogen had met at a party downtown—a party that she frequently liked to remind him she had almost skipped because her Labrador puppy had a cold that night.

Harry took another long, reflective drag of his cigarette. I tried to keep my body motionless but the involuntary canine trembling that many humans mistake for excitement made my collar tinkle.

Harry mistook the sound for bladder-based urgency. He took my leash down from the hook beside the door and clapped his big hands together.

"Want to go for a walk, boy?"

Harry employed the singsong voice reserved for inducing the delivery of a swift Number 1 or 2 by Yours Truly.

I sat down and let him snap the leash to my collar. I am fortunate in this important regard: he is sensitive to my need for walks, seldom inflicting a marathon of waiting that might force me to test my house-trained credentials.

It was well past midnight and our street was empty. It had stopped raining, but the sidewalk still glistened. Young Harry remained silent. He sucked the life out of his cigarette and lit a second. Together we exhaled great clouds of steam and smoke into the cold night air as we trotted toward Central Park. We crossed the avenue, passed through the park gate and down the tree-lined path. The ground was hard beneath my paws, but a little spongy in places from the rain. Indeed, it felt like December—winter but not quite.

My nose filled with an inexplicably rich array of winter smells. Smells are a central fact of my universe. I will do my best to share them with you despite the extreme differences in our noses which, to make a wine-tasting parallel, will reduce the finest vintage for you to a third-rate beer for me. What a marvelous organ! A Labrador's sense of smell is 100,000 times more acute than that of man. Imagine what the world would be like if humans could smell with the same complexity. Humans would have at their disposal a rich vocabulary that could illuminate nuance and shed truth. But more on that later.

Even in the absence of need, I never forget to pull Harry toward the little hill that has been designated for my Number 1s. I think if I act a bit Pavlovian it reinforces the importance of regular walks in my owner's mind. That night, I lifted my right leg and as usual felt embarrassed even though there was no one else about.

Not that Harry was paying me the slightest bit of attention. He was off with the pixies — sad and brokenhearted pixies.

"Sometimes," Harry said, "the spirits will call to us so strongly that our bodies just let us go. Maybe that's what happened to Overton. Maybe his first wife was calling from the beyond."

Malarkey, of course, but I couldn't blame Harry. Imogen had left us both quite alone, forced to pick up the fragments as best we could and lick wounds that showed no sign of healing. Harry had responded to her absence by opening himself up to people and ideas that Imogen would have promptly dismissed as fools and absurdities — and Harry would have felt the same confident disdain in happier times.

If Imogen's disappearance had taught me anything it was this: men need to be loved or they will slowly and invariably go bad. A perfectly adequate male in his twenties will become, in little more than a decade — if unloved — a strange creature statistically prone to die of an ingrown toenail in an apartment crammed with hoarded newspapers and unwashed cereal bowls.

Harry wasn't the only male that could use Imogen's help. I was also slipping without her. She had been my mistress long before she had been Harry's. My mind scrolled backward five years.

"Aren't you a wise little dog?" Imogen had said, lifting my puppy body high in the air and gently flicking my chin, white even then. That very day she had whisked me away from the pet store clods, the sawdust and the poking children to my first home: a little studio in the East Village.

Imogen had made better males of us both and yet the anatomy of my dog's eyes would never permit me to shed a single tear for my vanished mistress.